THE THEORY OF DEVIANCE

REBECCA GRACE ALLEN

This is a work of fiction. Names, characters, places, and incidents are the product of the author's imagination or are used fictitiously. Any resemblance to actual events, locales, or persons, living or dead, is purely coincidental.

Rebecca Grace Allen Enterprises

The Theory of Deviance

Copyright © 2016 by Rebecca Grace Allen

Print ISBN: 978-0-9992066-1-4

Digital ISBN: 978-0-9978792-5-4

Editing by Jennifer Miller

First Samhain Publishing, Ltd. electronic and print publication: August 2016

CONTENTS

If it's dark, deviant, and wrong, why does it feel so right?

Aspiring actress Krissy Porter longs to feel normal again, to finally shed her stage fright and fear of failure. And what could be more normal than dating the sweet, gentle musician she met at her sister's wedding? Trouble is, she's not sure how to explain the complicated friends-with-benefits situation she has with her hetero-flexible roommate, Rafe.

Mikey Pelletier longs for a normal life, too. But as a painfully shy, closeted bisexual virgin, he's afraid that might not be in the cards for him. Winning the gorgeous Krissy's heart would solve a lot of his problems. If only he wasn't equally attracted to her sexy tattooed roommate.

A week trapped together in a snowstorm will give this threesome the opportunity to indulge in their deepest, darkest, most rebellious desires. But they'll have to slay their inner demons—and lose their fear of deviance—first.

The Theory of Deviance, book 3 in the Portland Rebels series, is an ugly duckling, MMF, ménage contemporary romance story that's deliciously steamy, surprisingly emotional, and unapologetically hot. If you're ready for this unconventional love story about a strong bipolar heroine and the oh-so-sexy *men* of her dreams, grab it today.

The Theory of Deviance. (ˈthirē of ˈdēvēƏns)

A theory that states that those who obey the rules and laws of life are controlled by things like social norms. Any behavior that violates the dominant culture can warrant disapproval, or be assertions of individuality and identity.

Rebel. (ˈrebƏl) Noun.

A person who resists rules or norms.

Defiant, disobedient.

Unruly.

Subverts authority, control, or tradition.

ONE

Mikey Pelletier shifted his weight from one foot to the other as he stood in the waiting room of the Portland Transportation Center. Almost ten at night on the Friday after Christmas, and dozens of people were milling around, waiting to retrieve or send off loved ones. The place was nothing special—checkerboard carpeting, fluorescent lighting, and row after row of those uncomfortable metal chairs—but nervous excitement slammed into Mikey nonetheless as he scanned the bay doors.

Weeks of planning had led to this moment, hours finagled, and overtime accrued, and now he was on the stay-cation he'd been waiting for. One with transportation that included heat as well as access to a parent-free landing pad, giving him a taste of the independence he desperately needed.

There was another thing he desperately needed, and he'd be seeing it soon in the form of Krissy Porter, the quirky college senior he'd met three months earlier.

The sign announcing her bus's arrival flickered to life, and Mikey's gut clenched with an uneasy mix of hope and anticipation and anxiety. He'd only spent a few days with Krissy when they first met, but she'd knocked him off his ass the second they were introduced.

It wasn't just because of how damn cute she was, five foot two with raven-black hair, bright blue eyes, and glasses bigger than his own. It was because she had this *energy* to her—always talking a mile a minute, fun and outgoing with the right amount of geeky thrown in.

He hadn't talked to her right away, of course, hadn't walked up to her with the kind of cocky self-confidence the friends who'd introduced them always had. Sure, he'd spent half his life living vicariously through his buddies' defiant behavior, but Mikey had never been much of a rebel. With eyes too dry for contact lenses, unruly hair, and a wiry frame that never managed to pack on much muscle no matter how much time he spent with a snow shovel or a bag of mulch, he'd always felt like the odd man out— an ugly duckling among cooler, better-looking swans. He never challenged authority, bowing out whenever conflict came his way. It was probably why he was still a virgin at twenty-five years old.

No, it was definitely why. But that was going to change this week.

At least, he hoped it would.

Nothing had happened between him and Krissy back in September, other than a walk along the beach and a last-minute invitation to be her date at the wedding that had been the reason for her visit. Their time together had ended with a quick kiss and a note she'd jammed in his hands asking him to call her. He'd barely waited a day before doing exactly that.

The three hundred and fifteen miles between his home in Maine and where she went to college at NYU Tisch had limited their conversations to text and Skype, but they'd been talking several times a week since. They hadn't gotten any face-to-face time recently because of her exams, but today she was coming back here again to see him.

His phone buzzed. Mikey pulled it from his pocket, smiling as the screen lit up with a message from her.

I need the bathroom right this second or I'm gonna die!!!!

Mikey exhaled on a chuckle. Krissy's silliness was one of his favorite things about her, and Lord knew he needed some humor in his life, especially given how tense shit had gotten at home.

Her bus parked beyond the double glass doors, and Mikey's limbs went tingly as he watched the passengers disembark. Shoving his hair out of his eyes, he stood up straighter and looked for her and the girl she was traveling with.

Krissy's companion was the only downside of the week: she was being accompanied by her roommate, both of them having vacated their Queens apartment in order to trade homes with Mikey's friend Dean and his girlfriend, Jamie.

It had been Dean's brilliant idea to do an apartment swap with Krissy, arranging a vacation-rental switch like the one in the movie *The Holiday*. Appropriate, considering the time of year. Jamie and Krissy weren't strangers though—they'd been family-by-marriage since Krissy's sister had wed Jamie's brother in the fall. Jamie had always wanted to visit Manhattan, and Dean knew Mikey was hung up on his missed opportunity with Krissy. A few phone calls later and boom, the plans were set in motion. Dean and Jamie were off to visit the Big Apple, and Krissy was spending her winter break in Portland.

Inviting her roommate along was a sacrifice Mikey hadn't wanted to make, but it was worth it if it got Krissy here. He wasn't sure what to expect from the coming days since neither of them had stated their interest in words, but he'd be a liar if he said he wasn't hoping for *something* to happen.

It was more than wanting to make his virginity a thing of the past, though. He needed the security that came with being involved with someone of the opposite sex.

Emphasis on *opposite*.

A bad taste found its way into Mikey's mouth, memories of the events that turned his life upside down twisting through his stomach like a tangle of weeds. He wasn't planning to share that part of his past with Krissy. The virgin thing would come up eventually, but telling her he'd fallen for a guy in college—the shock of a lifetime, considering he'd grown up thinking he was straight—was definitely off the agenda.

His lack of honesty was a deviation from the norm, but Mikey had learned his lesson. He'd told his parents, but they hadn't given him the support he'd hoped for. They still loved him, and weren't even all that shocked, it seemed. But they were more worried about the impact his queerness might have on the family business than they were about him, reminding him of their stake in the community and begging him not to "choose this lifestyle".

As if he'd had the option of choosing anything. Discovering he was bi wasn't something he would've asked for in the great cosmic multiple-choice list of shit to be born with.

But this week was an opportunity to put that behind him. To have the straight, normal relationship he wanted and live a nice, quiet life in this nice, quiet town, continue his job working for his parents and volunteering as the youth choir leader at his church.

Being raised Catholic had only made Mikey more confused when his sexual interests took a sudden one-eighty. The Bible was pretty clear on what was right or wrong when it came to homosexuality, and while Mikey hoped an almighty being could never be that exclusionary, he wasn't sure God would accept him if he gave in to his feelings about men either.

Feeling. Singular. It had only been the one time. He hadn't done anything about it anyway, so it was possible this same-sex attraction thing was all in his head and would vanish once he got some real action.

People began filing in, and Mikey did a double take when he caught sight of Krissy. Or at least, someone he thought was her. Same oval face, same tiny stature despite the puffy jacket she was wearing, but the hair spilling out of her furry hood was no longer black. It was a honey-brown color with lighter streaks framing her face. Her glasses were gone too.

The feeling that she'd changed from the girl he'd met was unnerving, but then she smiled and waved wildly at him, and Mikey's worries dissipated like warm breath on a morning freeze. That was Krissy, all right. Goofy as he remembered, and he had to admit, just as sexy without the glasses.

She did a little dance and pointed at the bathroom, her lips pinching into a grimace of obvious distress. Mikey laughed and nodded, gazing after her in confusion as she booked it down the hall. She was still striking even with the changes—a kind of Renaissance-era beauty, with strong cheekbones and a high forehead, a little more meat to her bones, and a face so expressive you couldn't help smiling when she did.

He didn't know why she'd altered her appearance, but she was a theater student after all. Maybe she'd done it for a role.

Waiting for her return, Mikey scanned the crowd, wondering who among them was her roommate. He didn't know what to be on the lookout for, since Krissy hadn't given him a description. All Mikey knew was that she was older, and that the two of them had met while performing in a show together. He figured he'd have to entertain the other girl some of the time, but prayed she'd be an understanding person. Alone time with Krissy was essential.

The door from the bus lane opened again, frigid air blasting in as a man held it open for the last group of passengers. With one large duffle bag hoisted over his shoulder and another gripped easily in his other hand, he strode into the room with confidence. Something that could only be described as a swagger.

A tingling chill raced up Mikey's spine. The guy was tall, with a styled crop of short brown hair. A thin, finely trimmed beard and sparse mustache were the perfect accessories to his diamond-shaped face. Dressed in a leather jacket, black boots, and a pair of jeans that outlined the ridiculous amount of long, lean muscle in between, this guy was everything Mikey wasn't.

And everything he wanted.

The guy's gaze swept across the room and landed on Mikey. Dark-blue eyes locked with his.

Shit.

Mikey soldered his jaw shut and turned to face the restrooms. Thoughts like those weren't welcome with Krissy around. Her presence here was a chance to change things. To prove his attraction to men was simply a factor of his virgin curiosity. To drive those desires from his mind, because Mikey was afraid if he didn't, hellfire and damnation were all that awaited him.

The women's room door flew open, and Krissy bounded out. She skipped across the room and gleefully wrapped her arms around him.

"Hi!" Her breath came out in a humid rush as she pecked his cheek with a light kiss. The tip of her nose was still cold.

"Hi back," he said, returning her hug.

Mikey barely cleared five-eight, but Krissy's size and the way her shoulders inched up as she snuggled closer made him feel tall enough for the NBA. She peered up at him, and Mikey's heartbeat stuttered as he gazed into her eyes. They were a dramatic violet now instead of the bright blue they'd been before. Colored contacts maybe? Or had he remembered the color wrong?

"You look..." He searched for a word. "Different."

She arched her brow. "*Good* different?"

The look on her face made him worry he'd offended her until she pursed her lips and grinned.

God, those lips. So full and soft, with a little cleft in her chin he wanted to run his thumb over, kiss her in the middle of this crowded bus station, if only he had the balls to do it.

Painful shyness. Another reason why Mikey was as pure as the driven snow. But he could at least manage to tell her he dug her new style.

"Good," he sputtered. "Definitely good."

"Thank you." She went up on her toes and whispered into his ear, "I was hoping you'd like it."

Mikey shivered, all his awareness on the feel of her mouth, on the intimacy of softly spoken words. He made a tentative squeeze at her hips, and the slightly mischievous gleam that appeared in her eyes had his heart racing.

"I'm so happy you're here," he said.

"Me too." Krissy stepped back and stretched her arms over her head. "Longest. Trip. Ever."

A duffle bag landed by their feet, followed by a deep chuckle. "You said it, sweetheart."

Mikey held himself still, like he'd just noticed a wild animal and was doing his best not to attract its attention. He slid his gaze sideways, but the slow movement didn't change the fact that the hot guy from the doorway was standing next to them.

"A subway ride into the city. Four and a half hours on a train, another sitting around Boston South Station and two more on a bus." The man dropped the other bag to the floor and rolled his shoulders. "We're chartering a plane home, Krissy. I don't care how much it costs."

"Yeah, because that's in our budget," she replied with a giggle.

Our budget? Mikey narrowed his eyes, gaze darting between them until Krissy gave him a sheepish grin.

"Oh man, I forgot to introduce you two. Rafe, this is Mikey. Mikey, this is my roommate, Rafe."

No. Please, no.

Rafe stuck a hand out. "Pleasure to meet you."

The heavy, sick weight of jealousy and disappointment slinked into Mikey's stomach. He'd thought Krissy's roommate was female, but a quick mental recount of their conversations proved she'd never given him any reason to think that at all. The guy was even better looking up close—he had the kind of model-quality good looks you'd see on those vampire TV shows where everyone had sex with everyone else—which made Mikey feel about ten times more intimidated and threatened. But he extended his own hand in a reflex anyway, a slow-motion move that made it feel like his arm was a separate entity from his body.

"Thanks. You too." He gave Rafe his best manly handshake. Despite the absence of gloves, Rafe's hand was hot, like he hadn't just been outside in subzero temperatures and was somehow lit by his own internal-combustion engine.

Mikey released Rafe's hand and looked to Krissy. "Ready to go?"

Her nod was accompanied by an enthusiastic, "Ready!"

Mikey glanced at Rafe and motioned to their bags. "You need a hand with those?"

Rafe slung the bigger of the two duffles effortlessly over his shoulder. "I've got it."

Of course he did.

The cold slammed into them as soon as they stepped outside, a blast of wind nearly forcing them back into the vestibule.

"Holy bejesus, it's freezing," Krissy said, and Mikey couldn't help but snicker.

Maine winters were harsh, the temperature barely climbing past the freezing mark from December to March, but the seasons were one of the things he loved most about it here. They were like their own life force, a living thing that gave each time of year character. Portland was a bit milder than the rest of the state—the climate was much more moderate along the coast. But it still snowed frequently, and there was a majesty to the ocean this time of year. The way the light hit the water in winter, creating a sparkle so intense you could feel how cold it was just by breathing... It reminded Mikey of a presence larger than himself.

The weather was also what kept Pelletier Property Services, his family's snow-removal and landscaping business, firmly in the black.

"You get used to it," he told her, then led them across the lot to a beat-up old Chevy pickup. It was Dean's truck, and being tasked with looking after it this week was nothing short of a godsend. Mikey drove a company vehicle for work, but he was off the clock this week, and the Schwinn he used to get around town the rest of the time didn't handle the icy roads well.

He unlocked the steel truck box on the flatbed, turning to Krissy as Rafe chucked their bags into it.

"You sure you're okay having me stay with you?" he asked quietly.

They'd talked about him crashing at Dean's the week before, since he felt responsible for Krissy while she was here, and Portland's closest METRO Bus stop was pretty far from the apartment. Dean had already given Mikey the green light to stay there—it was practically Mikey's second home as it was, his safe haven when things at home hit critical mass—but he still needed Krissy's okay.

"Of course," she said, and nodded toward Rafe. "I see this guy all the time. I came here to see you."

His distrust of the situation somewhat mollified, Mikey climbed into the driver's seat. Krissy slid between him and Rafe, and began a constant flow of questions as Mikey drove. How cold did it get here? Were there icebergs in the ocean? Did the waves ever actually freeze? It was like traveling with a very inquisitive child, but her curiosity was endearing. He'd almost relaxed by the time they reached their destination.

Almost.

"Nice place," Rafe murmured dryly.

His response didn't come as a surprise. The warehouse building by the harbor where Dean lived wasn't exactly a five-star hotel. The first floor housed the burgeoning car refurbishment line of the auto-body business he ran with his father, and the rickety outdoor staircase that led to the second-floor apartment often had Mikey saying a prayer for his safety.

"It's much nicer on the inside," he promised.

"It looks awesome," Krissy said. "And it's only one floor up, which is better than we can say for our place."

There was that word—*our* again. Another spark of envy flared in Mikey's gut, but it diminished when Krissy nudged her shoulder against his.

"I like it."

They gathered their things and made their way up the stairs, the wind whipping around them as they climbed. Less than a minute outside and Krissy was stomping her feet and rubbing her hands together. Mikey worked the key into the lock and opened the steel door leading inside.

"Here we are." He flicked on the lights, and the wide industrial loft filled with a warm glow.

"Are you shitting me?" Rafe asked. "This place is huge!" He dropped their bags to the floor and pulled off his coat. "Krissy, call Dean and Jamie. Tell them they can stay in New York. I'm never going back."

Hah. Told you.

"I'm glad you approve," Mikey said.

A minuscule turn of Rafe's head was followed by a quick

appraisal, Rafe's gaze flicking from Mikey's shoes to his face.
"I do."

Hold up. Had he been the recipient of a covert once-over, or
was it his imagination?

Rafe grinned wide, adding, "Exposed brick walls, hardwoods,
and floor-to-ceiling windows? It's like a little piece of heaven."

Definitely his imagination. Rafe's approval had been over the
apartment, not Mikey. And the fact that that bothered him...
bothered him.

"Okay, kids," Rafe said with a yawn. "I'm gonna give you
some alone time and hit the shower. Wash off some of this travel
grime." He bent down to retrieve the smaller of the two bags and
winked. "Bathroom?"

Mikey pointed him in the right direction. When Rafe had
closed the door behind him, Krissy reached for Mikey's hand.
She'd taken off her coat and tied her hair into a ponytail. Shorter
strands fell around her face, framing full cheeks still tinged with
pink from the cold. The long-sleeved, faded Mickey Mouse
thermal she was wearing rode up slightly, giving him a glimpse of
pale skin above her corduroys and brightly colored socks.

"You want to watch a movie or something?" she asked.

Relief fired through him. And a desire to touch her. "I'd
love to."

He grabbed the remote and had just flicked on the TV when
Krissy's cell phone rang.

"That'll be my parents, checking that I'm alive." She
retrieved her phone from her pocket. "Gotta report in. Sorry."

"No problem. Go ahead and take it in the bedroom. I'll find a
movie."

She grinned and hopped down the hall on the balls of her
feet, saying a singsong *"Hi Mom"* before the closed door muffled
her words.

Mikey flicked through the channels, stopping when he found *Home Alone*. Christmas might have been in their rearview mirror, but the holiday movies would be on until after New Year's.

He sat down on the futon that doubled as Dean's couch and busied himself with rearranging the pillows. He'd assumed he'd be sleeping here, at least the first night. The apartment only had one bedroom, and even though Dean had granted Mikey permission to make use of his king-size bed so long as he triple-washed the linens and blanket after, Mikey hadn't wanted to assume anything. At least not until he and Krissy got reacquainted.

Of course, it had all seemed simpler when he thought Krissy's roommate was female.

The shower flicked on, and Mikey bristled at the mere fact of Rafe's existence. He'd put so much stock into this week already, and the additional set of X-Y chromosomes currently hanging out in the bathroom was throwing another crapload of his insecurities into the mix. He had no clue what Krissy's relationship with Rafe was, or if the guy was competition. And why had he wanted Rafe's appreciation before? He was supposed to be jealous of him.

A few moments later, Krissy bounded from the bedroom and landed on the couch next to him.

"I love this movie!" she said, snuggling into his side.

He put an arm tentatively around her, glancing down at her feet as she got more comfortable. Her socks had monkeys printed on them, and fondness for her made some of Mikey's stress melt away. Krissy's style of dress was a little out there, but her mismatched combinations were another thing he liked about her. She was just as much an odd duck as he was, and that was a kinship he'd never shared with anyone.

The shower shut off after a while, followed by the bathroom door opening and the bedroom door closing. But Rafe didn't come out to join them, and Mikey didn't look a gift horse in the mouth wondering why. They'd barely gotten halfway through the movie when Krissy yawned—the hard, shuddery kind.

"Tired?" he asked.

She nodded. "Sorry. It's been a long day."

"Don't be sorry. This is nice, cuddling with you."

She put her head on his shoulder. By the time Kevin had sent the bad guys packing, she'd fallen asleep in his arms. Mikey let himself doze, enjoying the feel of her beside him. Of how *easy* it was, the way they fit together.

He hadn't realized he'd fallen asleep until he heard Rafe whispering her name.

"Kris, wake up," he said softly.

Mikey quirked one eye slightly open. Rafe was kneeling in front of them in sweats and a tank top, the muscles in his arms contoured by the low lamplight. It aggravated Mikey, seeing how much more attractive her roommate was with fewer clothes, as did Rafe's casual use of a nickname for Krissy. She stirred, lifting a hand to rub her eyes like a child. Rafe held out a bottle of water to her, as well as a small white pill.

A punch of unease landed in Mikey's gut but he kept still, limbs straining to hold his pose as he covertly watched Krissy take the tablet and swallow it with a drowsy smile. Neither of them looked at him as she curled back into Mikey's side. Rafe patted her thigh and left the room without another word.

What the hell?

Mikey had no idea what had just happened, but Krissy was already out cold again, so asking questions wasn't an option. Whatever Rafe had handed her, it had to be something innocuous, otherwise she wouldn't have taken it so easily, right?

He looked down at her sleeping form, her long lashes brushing her cheeks.

So much for the discussion on the sleeping arrangements.

He didn't want to take any liberties by sleeping with her uninvited, especially with her being so tired, but he figured her nuzzling up to him like this was a decent enough invitation.

Gently untangling himself, he urged her down onto her side and made what was probably the world's worst attempt to open a futon without waking someone. She somehow slept through it, and Mikey switched off the lights, eager to wrap himself around her.

He pulled off her shoes, then stepped out of his own and climbed onto the mattress beside her. Pulling the blanket over them, he took off his glasses and placed them on the arm of the couch. The world got fuzzy, but Krissy was clear, and he moved in close to her, hoping things would make more sense in the morning.

TWO

Bright sunlight pulled Krissy out of sleep. She forced her eyes open, but they were scratchy, her vision blurry. Awesome, she'd slept in her contacts again. And her clothes, apparently.

Sitting up, she blinked a few times until the sticky cloudiness cleared, then took in her unfamiliar surroundings. Big, open living room, single-wall kitchen taking up the far corner. Wide windows with a view of the ocean. Mikey asleep on the futon next to her.

Right. She was in Maine, at Jamie and Dean's apartment.

The usual vague sense of unease took hold, and Krissy did a mental check, canvassing recent events like a computer virus scan. It was like this every morning now—her mind speeding through worries that she'd forgotten an important assignment or something bad had happened. But nothing had gone wrong in the last twenty-four hours. She was on vacation, away from the pressures of family and school, and here to see Mikey.

Krissy glanced down at him, and the knot of anxiety in her chest loosened. He must've tucked her in last night, even though she had no memory of being covered by the blanket that was wrapped around her, or anything past about midway through the movie. She'd tried to stay awake for the end—she always liked the part when Kevin's neighbor reunited with his granddaughter—but she must've needed to sleep. Still catching up on the last few days, she guessed.

Had she taken her meds?

Her lungs went tight on a sharp breath, but then she recalled Rafe coaxing her pill into her hands. Mikey had fallen asleep watching the movie too—she remembered that much at least—and hopefully hadn't noticed.

He might notice the sound of her alarm going off though.

After slipping out from underneath the blanket, she scurried down the hall. The sound of her phone beeping got louder when she reached the bedroom. Rafe was an immobile form under the covers, barely visible except for the top of his head. She located her phone, plugged in and charging where it sat atop her bag. Rewetting solution and cleanser for her contacts were on the floor next to it.

Trust Rafe to take care of things. He always did.

She picked up her phone and swiped right to turn off the alarm. A reminder alert with a smiley face on it popped up.

You haven't logged your mood yet. How are you feeling right now?

With a small sense of achievement, Krissy began the routine she'd become accustomed to. Opening the mood journal app, she chose "good" from the scale listed on the screen. There, easy-peasy. The trip hadn't thrown her out of whack like her therapist had warned. Sure, she'd missed her yoga practice yesterday, but she'd caught up on her sleep last night and would do double with the stretches today.

Trying not to disturb Rafe, she grabbed her toiletries and tiptoed toward the door. A rustling stopped her in her tracks.

"Are you going to tell him?"

Krissy froze, her hand on the knob. "Tell him what?"

Even without looking, she could see Rafe rolling his eyes. "Kris..."

She sighed. "I know. I will. Let me see how things go first."

He replied with a grunt before turning over. "Wake me when there's coffee."

Krissy went into the bathroom, popped out her contacts, and rinsed them with solution. She couldn't see what she was doing, but her glasses were in her bag, and she didn't feel like going back into the bedroom to fish them out. After fumbling with putting the lenses back in, she brushed her teeth and hair, then padded out to the living room. Mikey sat up as soon as she came in.

"Hey." He reached for his glasses and slipped them onto his face. "I didn't hear you get up."

Lord, he was adorable. Messy dark hair. Sideburns that made him look like a young Hugh Grant. Yeah, his glasses screamed Clark Kent, but she had the feeling it was Superman who lurked beneath the surface.

"I've only been up a few minutes. Sorry I conked out last night."

She braced her palms on the back of the armchair and went up and down on her toes. The flex-and-point habit had become ingrained in her after years of ballet. She'd stopped training in high school, her time filled instead with voice lessons and drama club, but it had become her go-to practice when she was too antsy to keep still. Like now.

"It's okay. You'd had a long day," he said. "You hungry?"

Her stomach grumbled, or maybe it had been grumbling for a while and she hadn't noticed. She hadn't eaten since their stopover in Boston. Not a good thing, but an easy fix.

"Starving."

"We could make pancakes. I bought some local maple syrup yesterday."

"That sounds awesome!"

An over-the-top reaction, but Mikey didn't blink, and something that had been wound too tight inside her slackened. This was what had attracted her to him when they met; he never looked at her strangely, never flinched at her occasionally strange behavior the way so many other people had.

The way so many people who were supposed to love her *still* did.

Mikey started to move, then stopped and balled a fist in the blanket over his lap. "I just need to..." His cheeks tinged with pink. "You get the coffee going, okay? I'll be right back."

Krissy stood mutely for a second, then caught the placement of his hand.

"Oh! Yeah. Go ahead. I'll...be in here."

She walked toward the kitchen, peering over her shoulder as Mikey sped toward the bathroom. Was his hurry because he needed to pee, or was there something of the morning-wood variety that he had to take care of?

If it was the latter, she would've liked to help him out with that.

Snickering, she searched through the cabinets until she found a bag of Green Mountain coffee. The machine had gurgled its way through half a pot by the time Mikey joined her a few minutes later. They began the preparations, mixing ingredients until thick batter was sizzling on a pan.

"What did you have in mind for today?" she asked.

"I thought maybe a tour of Portland? We could drive around, then head to the Old Port for dinner." He paused. "Will Rafe be joining us?"

Mikey's tone changed with the question, tension appearing in the little divot between his brows. The knot reformed in Krissy's chest. She should've clued him in earlier about Rafe. She'd felt like an imposter, leaving out important details about her roommate every time she and Mikey chatted, but that was her life—a carefully constructed web of different lies to different people, keeping them safe from the truth she was sure no one would understand.

"Probably. Assuming he doesn't spend the day sending harassing emails to his agent." She said it with humor, but Mikey didn't laugh. "Is that all right?"

"Yeah. Of course. Totally fine," he said, nodding quickly. "You two are close?"

Understatement of the year, but whatever. "He's—" she searched for the right words, "—my best friend."

Mikey's gaze remained fixed on the food. "Can I ask you..."

Krissy held perfectly still, guarding herself against his impending question. *Please don't go there. Not about Rafe. Not yet.* But all he did was shake his head and smile.

"No, forget it. It's none of my business." He slid a spatula under each pancake and began piling them on a platter as he jutted his chin toward a cabinet. "Would you mind setting the table? Plates and cups are in there."

Gathering as much as she could, Krissy carried three settings to the table. By the time she'd folded the last napkin, Mikey was by her side with the platter of food. He placed it on the table and sat next to her.

"You slept okay last night?" he asked. "It was all right on the futon?"

"With you, you mean?" She grinned, and Mikey blushed again. "Yes, it was definitely okay. Was it okay with you?" She meant to let him answer, but the words kept coming, rushing out like a waterfall. "I'm really sorry I passed out on you. I can be dead to the world when I haven't slept enough. This week was super busy, running out to my parents' house for the holidays, then going back home and getting ready for this trip."

She was talking so fast she needed to catch her breath. *Slow your roll, Krissy.*

"Is it a long ride?"

"It's not too bad. A quick subway trip into the city, and Metro North goes straight from there to Connecticut." Krissy shrugged. "Just one of the hazards of being a B and T."

"B and T?"

"A 'bridge and tunnel' person," she explained. "It's a nickname for people who live in the other boroughs and have to take a bridge or a tunnel to get anywhere. Commuting is a pain in the ass, but Queens is less expensive than Manhattan, so it's worth it."

He nodded. It was funny, all the little things about their lives they hadn't talked about before. Mundane details that suddenly filled an awkward silence she feared had been fueled by unanswered questions.

They filled their plates with food, no sound between them except for the clinking of silverware against ceramic until Mikey finally asked, "You had a good Christmas?"

Krissy hesitated before answering. Her parents were an interfaith couple. They didn't belong to a church or a temple and had introduced Krissy and her sister, Kim, to the Old and New Testaments as children, bedtime stories that had been so interspersed with fairy tales Krissy couldn't tell them apart anymore. But religion was important to Mikey—at least it seemed so, given the fact that he volunteered at his church—so she wanted to tread lightly.

"We're not religious, but my Dad's side celebrates Christmas, so we spend it with them." Krissy's stomach growled, reminding her how hungry she was. She poured a generous serving of syrup onto her pancakes. "What about you?"

"It was good. Had Christmas dinner with my extended family. Christmas Eve I was working though. Took the choir caroling."

She loved the image that popped into her head—Mikey surrounded by children in mittens and earmuffs, conducting them as they sang "Jingle Bells" on doorsteps.

"Did you go from house to house?"

"We made a stop at a park in the neighborhood, but the big performances were at the hospital and nursing home."

"You like the church job?" She knew he took working for his family's company seriously, but the musical post seemed to suit him better. "I know you said it didn't pay, but is that what you'd rather be doing?"

Mikey made a sound that was half a laugh, half a cough. Crap. She'd been asking too many questions. It was a reflex, though. When you asked people a lot of stuff, it stopped them from asking anything about you.

"It's just a fun thing I do on the side," he said. "I only took the position because I was in the choir as a kid. I knew the former director, and he asked me if I'd be willing to fill his role when he left. But I like working in nature. Taking care of things. It's why I majored in environmental studies—for me and for my parents' business."

The last line made it seem more like he was convincing himself of the answer more than anything else, but Krissy didn't push it.

"Got it." She tucked into her breakfast, took her first bite, and moaned.

Mikey grinned around his own mouthful of food. "Good?"

"Good doesn't begin to cover it!" She downed another forkful and moaned again. "Swear to God, this is better than sex."

Mikey nearly choked around his swallow. "Is it?"

It'd been a while since she'd done the actual deed, but she'd certainly classify this combination of fluffy, rich, and sweet as orgasmic. She gazed at him from beneath lowered lashes.

"Absolutely. Should I expect everything you get your hands on to be this good?"

Mikey's blush was coupled with a shy glance at his plate. Two dimples pushed at the edges of his pink lips as they curled upward. The slightly feminine shape of his mouth provided a lovely contrast to his square jaw. He leaned closer, and electricity sparked between them in the cold morning air.

Oh, yes. She might have come here riddled with skepticism, doubting what she'd felt during those few short days they'd spent together, but *this*. This was what she wanted—the flirting, the connection, excitement buzzing inside her like the moment before a curtain lifts and pretending for a short time that she could have something real.

"Are those pancakes I smell?" Rafe called out.

Krissy glanced over her shoulder, and the thrill Mikey's reaction had shot through her intensified. Dressed in nothing but rumpled black sweats and a charcoal tank top that showed off his upper body, her roommate looked as sex-mussed as he always did first thing in the morning.

That was Rafe. Ready-made sex appeal. Just add water.

"They are," Krissy replied, telling herself that Rafe's interruption was a good thing. Getting her hopes up with Mikey this soon was a bad idea. "Grab a plate before I eat yours too."

Rafe made himself a heaping serving and sat down across from them.

"So," he drawled as he poured syrup directly onto a spoon and lazily sucked it off. "What's on tap for today?"

There was a brief pause before Mikey answered, his body taut and closed off. Krissy had some ruffled feathers to smooth here, but that was a juggling act she'd figure out how to balance later. Mikey went through options on what the tour highlights could be, and they decided on a plan. When he stood to clear his place, Rafe made a pointed glance at her. A look that clearly said *did you tell him yet?*

Krissy ignored him. Hopping out of her seat, she brought her dish and mug to the sink. "I call dibs on the shower," she hollered, then raced toward the bathroom.

Locking the door behind her, Krissy silently scolded Rafe, even though she knew he was only trying to help. She had to come clean if she wanted something more than friendship with Mikey, but seriously, how the hell was she supposed to do that?

"Hey, I know this might sound crazy, but..."

No. Her therapist had instructed her not to use the C-word. She had bipolar disorder and needed to talk about it the same way she would a medical illness. But her diagnosis carried a huge stigma, and her experiences with telling people about it hadn't usually ended well.

Sighing as she stepped into the shower, Krissy soaped her legs and grabbed her razor. She hadn't expected anything to come from this week. Sure, she'd been "Mikey this, Mikey that" since she'd come back from Maine, but she couldn't trust her feelings. Intense and brief connections were a factor of her condition. Now that she was here again, the bond they'd formed *seemed* real, but things would change when she told him the whole saga. Once he knew what had gone down at school, the trail of disaster she'd left in her wake, and the things she had to do now to keep herself on an even keel, he'd run for the hills.

But say he didn't? Then what? She was too messed up to be anybody's girlfriend. Keeping her emotions in check was hard enough without adding in the roller coaster of a relationship. It was why she'd spent the last two years avoiding being intimate with anyone.

Make that, almost anyone.

Krissy stared down at the line she'd drawn through the foam

on her legs. Her relationship with Rafe was as complicated and delicate as her mental state, which was ironic since it was the only thing that had kept her sane.

They didn't sleep together; he'd drawn a line in the sand over intercourse that Krissy never wanted to push. Sex made things more serious, he'd said, and while Rafe went both ways in the bedroom, his heart swayed more toward men.

It was fine. She didn't love him *that* way, not fully anyway, and their play was one of the many ways he took care of her. Fooling around with him stuck a literal finger in the dam of her raging libido, no complicated feelings required.

It had worked out fine in the beginning, but after a while she'd noticed him getting twitchy. A longing look at an attractive man when they grabbed dinner somewhere. A night out at a gay bar that ended with him coming home cranky and alone. She'd finally told him to please go out and get his. It was fine with her if he hooked up with a guy, as long as he stayed safe. She wouldn't be jealous.

Actually, she found it pretty damn hot.

If he'd done so, he didn't say. Maybe he had and kept quiet about it because he didn't want to hurt her. She knew what they were doing wasn't healthy, and it couldn't go on forever, which was why Rafe was all about her taking a shot at things with Mikey this week. But explaining this to him was going to be impossible.

God, she wished she could just be *normal*, instead of having a body and brain chemistry that constantly rebelled against it.

She'd tell Mikey the truth, but not yet. They had a fun day planned ahead of them, and Krissy wanted to enjoy it for as long as she could.

* * *

IT WAS past midday by the time they'd rotated shifts in the shower and headed outside. The chunky rainbow-striped tights and vintage corduroy dress Krissy had on beneath her jacket didn't keep her very warm, and she gunned it for the truck, climbing inside as soon as Mikey unlocked it. The engine rumbled to life, heat sputtering through the vents as they set off down the street.

The buildings became more residential farther down the road, and they came upon a large church with a huge steeple. Tall, ornate windows were set in green wrought-iron casings. Broad cement steps led to three sets of double doors, balsam wreaths with red bows hanging from each one.

Mikey nodded toward it. "That's my family's church. Where I work."

"You work at a *church?*" Rafe spat. "I thought you were a landscaper."

Krissy winced. Rafe and religion didn't exactly see eye to eye, and Mikey's second job was one more thing she hadn't found a way to explain yet.

"It's a volunteer gig, part time," she said. "He's the musical director. Teaches the kids. Right, Mikey?"

He responded with a tight nod. An uncomfortable silence filled the cab.

Awwwwkward.

Krissy fiddled with the radio, compelled to cover for Rafe's glaring disdain and the distance that settled between them. One hand squeezing Rafe's in apology, she searched through stations and asked Mikey about different landmarks. He eventually loosened up, noting some of the houses he'd worked on and pointing out a Pelletier Property Services truck when they passed it. Rafe finally patted her knee, and the silent acknowledgement let Krissy relax enough to enjoy her surroundings.

New England charm was everywhere, from the colonial

architecture to the beach snack bar shut up tight for the season, its walls decorated with colorful lobster buoys that were dusted with a fine layer of snow. Maine might've been gripped by the depths of winter, but it was beautiful nonetheless. Rays of orange-gold sunlight reflected on the snow, making everything shimmer and sparkle. Chunks of ice idled in the harbor, bobbing on deep blue water.

"I totally dig the vibe here," she said when they made their way across the bridge into the Old Port. Cobblestone streets made parallel lines along the wooden structure of the wharf, warehouses from another era renovated to incorporate shops, galleries, and restaurants. With sparkling white lights in the trees and snowflake decorations on every storefront, the town was painted like a classic Christmas card picture. "It's like a more chill, festive Greenwich Village."

"You know there are a few theaters here," Rafe said. "You can audition after you graduate."

Mikey glanced in her direction. "You're thinking about moving here?"

"I dunno. Maybe?" It was a fleeting thought she'd had, not one she was ready to take seriously. Krissy elbowed Rafe, but he wasn't deterred.

"She's trying to decide what to do after graduation," he told Mikey. "I said she's nuts to want to get into acting at all, but why should she listen to me, someone who knows how fickle life in the theater can be."

She elbowed him again, but he grabbed her arm and held her still, answering her glare with a wag of his eyebrows.

Pain in the ass.

"Rafe's in between shows," she explained. "His last one closed in November. He had a bunch of auditions last week. It's why he's jumping every time his email dings."

"Ergo, I know what I'm talking about. Get out now, while you still can."

He released her elbow and poked her side until she giggled and squirmed. The move pushed her closer to Mikey, and Krissy tried not to react to the contact, too many body parts in such close proximity.

"I love the theater," she said once she'd recovered. "Access to costuming means an easy way to keep adding to my fabulous wardrobe."

She smoothed down her dress, an item found in a bin of unwanted costumes at school. Theater dumpster-diving was a habit of hers during set break-downs, the more eccentric the better. It was fun, feeling like she was always a little in character.

"Well, you'd better make some decisions soon," Rafe said. "The clock is ticking."

"Really?" She stuck out her tongue at him. "I hadn't realized."

She didn't need the reminder. Her family kept at it enough for them all.

Five months until she finished school, and Krissy hadn't made any solid plans. It wasn't for lack of love of the stage—it was just hard to figure out what she wanted, especially with Rafe and her parents telling her what was best all the time. But she'd worked hard to keep up, needing to prove that she wasn't going back on her plans. She was going to be an actress, was going to graduate Tisch with a degree in drama, bipolar be damned.

She had to show her family she was capable of being the person she was before she got sick, so they would stop looking at her the way they did.

"My friend Merrick is in the area, performing with a local repertory company," Rafe continued. "He can get us comp tickets to a matinee tomorrow. Let you see how good their shows are."

He threw her an innocent grin. "Say the word, and I'll make it happen."

Krissy glanced at Mikey. "Would you like to do that?"

"If you want to, then sure."

There he went again, being so wonderfully unassuming and quiet. Not shoving ideas down her throat like everyone else did.

"Okay then," Rafe said. "I'll set it up."

He pulled out his phone and spent the remainder of the drive on it, only chiming in when the sun began creeping toward the horizon and Mikey asked if anyone was hungry.

"Sustenance would definitely be appreciated," Rafe said.

"Retweet!" Krissy needed to eat again, and soon. A big breakfast meant she hadn't been hungry for lunch, but regular meals were another part of the keeping-Krissy-from-going-off-the-deep-end agenda.

"Any requests?" Mikey asked.

She clapped her hands. "Can we go somewhere with lobster?"

"It's Maine," he replied with a laugh. "Every restaurant has lobster. But I know a nice place nearby."

He pulled up in front of a redbrick building on the waterfront. It was busy inside, the crowd within visible through several large windows. Rafe reached for the truck's door handle.

"I'll put our names down. You guys take your time finding parking." He winked at Krissy before hopping out.

It was a thinly veiled offering of time alone to talk. Well played, Rafe. Well played.

Nerves fluttering, Krissy practiced her yoga breathing as Mikey searched for a spot. He found one a block and a half up, shut off the ignition, and glanced over at her.

"Hey," he said softly. "Are you having fun?"

His eyes searched hers, big and brown and gentle. Awareness

prickled. She'd been holding herself back, but sitting with him in the quiet of the cab, the allure of being hidden in the shadows...

She shifted closer on the seat. "Yes. Are you?"

"Yes." A small smile turned up the corners of his mouth. "I like your hair, by the way. And your eyes. The color, I mean."

Relief washed the tension from her body. Coloring her hair had been a whim during finals week when she was too wound up to sleep, the purple contacts a spontaneous decision the morning after. She'd regretted it afterward, unsure of her choices as always, but Mikey's compliment felt like a standing ovation.

"I like *you*," she said.

He blinked. Stared at her lips. Licked his own. "I like you too."

Krissy's pulse raced. They were close, close enough to kiss. Close enough to forget about secrets and illnesses and have it all disappear under the hot slip of mouths and tongues.

Kiss me kiss me kiss me.

The high-pitched sound of her phone ringing startled her. Krissy pulled it from her purse with a groan. Mom and Dad checking in, of course. She could ignore it, but if she didn't answer, they'd probably call the police.

"Sorry. Just a sec," she told Mikey, then swiped the screen to answer. "Hey, Mom. Can I call you back?"

"Sure," her mother replied. "I just wanted to see if you were having a nice time."

"Yup, great time."

She promised to continue the conversation in a few, impatient to return her focus to Mikey, but by the time she ended the call, the moment was over.

THREE

Mikey figured it wasn't gentlemanly to kiss Krissy right after she got off the phone with her parents. He wanted to, because good *Lord* she was the perfect combination of cute and hot in her little puffy jacket, but not here. Not in the cab of a truck where anyone could notice.

And not with Rafe sitting in the restaurant, waiting for them.

"Let's get inside," he said. "It's cold, and you're hungry."

"Oh *man*, you're right. I'm starving. Let's go!"

She booked it out of the truck with a surge of energy he hadn't expected. Mikey led her down Fore Street, his stomach churning in anticipation of another meal with Rafe. Her roommate's presence was still unnerving. He didn't trust the guy, and the almost twenty-four hours of nonstop discomfort had made Mikey forget how attracted he'd been to Rafe when he first saw him.

Mostly.

Watching Rafe eat breakfast this morning had been like a trial from God. Each time he'd drizzled syrup on his spoon and sucked it off, Mikey's treacherous body reacted—pants going tight as he idly wondered what Rafe would look like if he were about to feast on things other than food.

Mikey hated it, not being able to block out those thoughts. This was his opportunity to make things work with Krissy. He wasn't supposed to be feeling like...*this*.

When they reached the restaurant's door, Mikey opened it for Krissy and followed her inside. It was a place he'd hoped to take her—a good blend of local fare and gourmet concoctions, the decor an eclectic mix of modern and Down-East style. Wrought-iron candelabras hung from wooden beams, sconces on the walls, and the open kitchen gave it a warm, homey feel.

They checked in with the hostess, who'd already seated Rafe in a booth by the windows.

"After you," he said to Krissy, but she palmed her phone and waved it in front of him.

"I've gotta call the parental units back first. You go ahead. I'll be right there."

She pecked him on the cheek and went off in the direction of the restrooms.

Mikey gazed after her, his stomach taking even more of a beating, his frustration and anxiety like a buzz saw to his nerves. But he squared his shoulders anyway, walked toward the table, and slid onto the bench seat opposite Rafe.

"Krissy had to call her parents," Mikey said.

Rafe didn't look up from the menu. "I swear, if those people could install GPS in her, they would."

So he'd met her family then. "They're super protective?"

"That's putting it mildly."

Another barb of jealousy jabbed at Mikey's sternum. He didn't like how well Rafe knew Krissy, how involved he was in her life. And that pill thing from last night was still bugging him. He'd wanted to talk to Krissy about it today, but how did you ask something like that? And it wasn't like he'd had a private moment to do so anyway, with Rafe along for the ride.

The server arrived with their waters and a basket of breadsticks. Rafe snatched one and munched nonchalantly, still reading the menu. Mikey took off his jacket and glared at Rafe, shoving his hair out of his eyes when it fell over his forehead again. He resented Rafe's presence, not to mention the feelings it had kicked up. And it was impossible to believe the guy didn't have some kind of designs on Krissy.

Mikey wasn't sure if it was some kind of primitive caveman impulse, but he felt the need to challenge Rafe. To prove he was a worthwhile candidate for Krissy's attention.

The quiet stretched on, the same edgy silence they'd had in the car, until he finally blurted, "I'm more than a landscaper, you know."

Rafe glanced up, one eyebrow lifted in amusement. "O-kay..."

The glib expression pissed Mikey off. He had something to prove here.

"We do full-on property management. Snow removal, spring and fall cleanups, lawn care, patio installation. That kind of stuff," he said. "And what's your problem with the church job? Some people actually like being a part of their religious community."

Rafe held up his hands in surrender. "Hey. Chill. I didn't mean anything by it, I swear. I was just surprised because Krissy hadn't mentioned it."

Mikey huffed out a breath, suddenly embarrassed he'd gotten so aggravated. The rise in temper was out of character for him. He'd always opted for flight instead of fight. Even when his parents got on his case about the whole dating thing, pleading with him to not make things harder for himself and to *"just stick with girls, since you like them too*", he headed for Dean's instead of arguing with them.

"Sorry," he said.

Rafe's smile hadn't dulled. "No worries." He lowered his hands and plucked another breadstick from the basket. "Honestly, I was really just shocked Krissy left anything out, with the way she hasn't stopped talking about you."

Hope flared in Mikey's chest. "She hasn't?"

Dark brows pressed together in a look of sympathetic mockery. "Duh." Rafe offered him a devious grin. "You like her, don't you."

Mikey's cheeks went hot. "Duh."

"Good. Then this week will go swimmingly."

Okay, so Rafe wanted him and Krissy together. Maybe the guy wasn't all bad. Mikey exhaled, returning a more muted version of Rafe's grin. His defensiveness seemed unfounded now that it didn't appear Rafe was a threat. The rest...well, that was in his head. He could bury it.

He had plenty of practice, after all. He'd been doing it for years.

"About the church job," Rafe said around a bite of cracker. "Are you...religious?"

"Sure. I mean, I'm not on my way to the Vatican or anything, but it's an important part of my life." Mikey glanced away, hoping Rafe couldn't hear the hypocrisy in his words.

As a child, he'd loved everything about his church: the rituals of mass and communion, the safe, reliable routine of tradition. He'd accepted the teachings in the Bible too but had questioned them as he got older, especially when he got to college and found himself lusting after the wrong kind of flesh. Wanting a man went against everything he'd been taught. He'd had friends at school who scoffed at the idea of it being a sin, even attended a few of the on-campus's Queer-Straight Alliance meetings at their prompting, but he couldn't shake the feeling that he'd put a blot on his soul.

Volunteering as the choir director made Mikey feel like he was at least doing *something* right. Like he was keeping a promise to God that he was a good person, even if the fantasies that still plagued him made him fear otherwise.

"The job isn't really a religious thing. I only work with the clergy when I need to plan music for the services."

"Gotcha," Rafe said. A glance in Krissy's direction was followed by another small lull in conversation. "You've lived in Maine all your life?"

"All my life."

"You like it here?"

"I do. It's nice, especially around the holidays, and my family's business is a big part of the community. It's impossible to feel lonely, living someplace where everybody knows you."

More hypocrisy. The Pelletiers' local celebrity status was the driving force behind his family's arguments. And Mikey had never felt lonelier. All his closest friends had paired up—Dean was with Jamie, their other buddy Connor was out in Boston helping his fiancée Gabriella pack to move here, and Mikey was starting to worry he'd be spending the rest of his days alone.

Rafe crunched on the breadstick, dark eyes still fixed on him. Mikey fidgeted under the other man's stare and said, "I guess that kind of life isn't for everyone."

Rafe huffed out a breath. "It certainly wasn't for me."

"You're not originally from Queens?" He imagined Rafe born with a New Yorker's street smarts, the kind of toughness you could only learn by living in a city filled with over eight million people.

The amusement on Rafe's face faded, replaced by a casual expression of indifference. "I'm from the South," he replied mildly. "Georgia."

"Wow. I'd never have known. You don't have an accent."

Rafe laughed—a short, bitter sound. "I hope not. I spent a shit-ton of cash on a dialect coach to get rid of it."

There was a haunted, faraway look in Rafe's eyes, but it disappeared when Krissy bounded back to their table and plopped into the spot beside Mikey.

"We can all relax now," she said, tugging off her jacket. "My parents have been temporarily placated."

"Are they worried about you not being safe?" Mikey asked.

Krissy paused, her nose scrunching up. "It's a long story."

Rafe snorted and rolled his eyes. Clearly there was more to this, but Mikey knew what it was like to not want to discuss stuff when you weren't ready. He was keeping things to himself too.

"I understand," he said, and the way Krissy beamed at him warmed Mikey like sunlight on a cold day.

The server returned, and Krissy quickly perused her choices, insisting the two of them go first. They ordered a bevy of seafood, and Mikey promised to share some of his fisherman's platter with her when it seemed to sway her decision to get the typical Maine standards of clam chowder and a lobster roll.

The server stepped away, and Mikey forced himself to start asking questions.

"So how did you two meet?" If there was a shot at him being more comfortable, he needed all the information he could get. "You said you were in a show?"

Krissy started fiddling with her straw wrapper. "Yes, the summer after my sophomore year."

"At Tisch?"

She shook her head. "No, Rafe was a few years ahead of me, and this show was *way* too risqué to be NYU approved."

And there went the becoming-more-comfortable portion of the program. "Risqué?"

Krissy ducked her head. She hid her face behind her hair, apparently too flustered to answer.

Rafe leaned in instead, arms crossing over the table, and Mikey's stomach flip-flopped at the slightly sinister lift of the other man's brow.

"The show was called 'The Theory of Deviance'," he said. "Written and directed by one of my friends who minored in psych. It was one of those too-smart-for-its-own-good, socially expressive plays showcasing behavior that violates societal norms. How people are born deviant but try to rise above it, not following through on their desires because of things like values, morality, religion." Rafe chuckled, dark eyes flashing. "It's a real theory about human behavior, but my buddy pushed the envelope with his interpretation. No Equity actors worth their salt were coming out for auditions, so I went back to my alma mater and put up a flyer."

He looked over at Krissy, and his gaze softened in a way that made jealousy spark once again in Mikey's gut. "This one showed up and was cast in a scene about a threesome."

The spark switched from envy to arousal. "With girls, or... guys?"

Krissy rubbed her lips together. Mikey stared at her mouth for a moment, mesmerized.

"Guys," she said, and Mikey tried to will away the semi pressing against his zipper. "But it was just acting. We weren't actually *doing* anything, although I did freak out a bit during the audition." She laughed and blushed. "I had no idea what I was getting myself into. *Someone* had to talk me down."

Rafe snickered. They exchanged glances, but before Mikey's jealousy had a chance to go from simmer to boil, Krissy turned his way.

"It was a short run. Only two weekends of performances. I

didn't even tell my family about it. I just did it hoping it would get me over my stage fright. Didn't really work though."

"You have stage fright?" Mikey asked. She was so outgoing, he couldn't imagine her being intimidated by anything.

Krissy wove the wrapper around her fingers. "I've been dancing forever so I can do that okay, but my acting skills aren't great and my voice needs serious work."

"She's wrong," Rafe said.

"I'm not."

"You are."

"Whatever." Krissy dropped the wrapper and rolled her eyes, but Rafe was smiling at her.

"She has an amazing voice," he said. "It's the only reason I haven't tried to scare her off acting entirely. She'll probably get a lead somewhere right out of college, which is more than I can say for myself."

"You'll get another show," Krissy insisted. Their banter was like watching a tennis match, something Mikey wasn't involved in until she glanced up at him. "Mikey sings, you know. Not only for the church job. He minored in music at school."

Now it was Mikey's turn to blush. "I only sing when I'm teaching. Mostly I play guitar."

"You never wanted to perform?" Rafe asked.

"Nah, just love music. The first time I sang in four-part harmony, I thought I'd witnessed a miracle."

Rafe's lips turned up at the edges. It was the same fond grin he'd given Krissy. "Now that, I understand."

He looked away, but the echo of his smile remained in Mikey's vision.

The server returned with their meals. Krissy cooed over the food, insisting on trying a bit of everyone's before starting a full-on inquisition about the local lobstering business. Mikey wasn't an expert on the subject, but he knew enough, and by the time they'd finished eating, she'd decided she wanted a trap of her own to bring home with her.

"We could go fishing in the Hudson," she said when they drove back to the apartment. "There might be untapped resources. Ones nobody knows about. We'd make a killing!"

Her unbridled enthusiasm was charming. She was a whirling dervish of energy, taking the stairs two at a time and hollering from the landing that she'd beat them.

Once they'd gotten inside and hung up their coats, Rafe collapsed onto the armchair. "The night's still young. What's next?"

Mikey had hoped *next* would be Rafe leaving him and Krissy alone again.

No such luck, apparently. But Mikey didn't want to be rude.

"We can watch another movie," he said, then nodded to Dean and Jamie's new collection of board games, the Christmas-slash-thank-you-for-this-week gift he'd given them. "Or play one of those?"

"Actually," Krissy said. "Would it be okay if I did yoga for a bit?"

She'd told him about her daily practice. He admired her diligence, even though he'd never been a fan of exercise himself. Dean had gotten into lifting lately and had invited Mikey to join, but that sounded about as appealing as a root canal after long days spent doing manual labor.

Krissy working out was different though. He would've preferred to be spending quality time with her, but watching her bend and stretch would be kinda hot.

"Sure," he said. "I'll move the table so you have room."

She skipped off to the bedroom to change. Rafe remained in the chair and pulled out his phone again while Mikey maneuvered furniture around.

"You need help with that?" Rafe asked distractedly.

"Got it," Mikey grunted. He might not have muscles to spare, but he could move a table two feet, thank you very much.

Krissy emerged from the bedroom a few minutes later, barefoot in bright pink leggings and an oversized purple shirt that said "Yoga Girls are Twisted".

Mikey snickered at the logo, only stealing a glance at the rest of her body after she'd plugged in her ear buds and bent down to unroll her mat. Tiny waist. Shapely hips and thighs, calves strong from her dance training, her body a perfect hourglass shape. Why had he passed up the opportunity to kiss her earlier?

Oh, right. Because he was a stupid, stupid nice guy. And because of other things. Things sitting in the middle of the living room.

Knowing he needed to keep himself busy for a while, Mikey retrieved his guitar from its spot in the corner. He'd brought it over yesterday, hoping he'd get to show Krissy some of the new stuff he was working on for the choir. He sat down on the futon, took a few minutes to tune it, then began plucking out the notes of R.E.M.'s "Losing My Religion".

Mikey's musical tastes were varied—everything from pop to alternative to country, although the last had always been his favorite. He thought the kids would get into this song though, and hummed along as he played, making mental notes of where he could split the group. He started singing at the chorus, and Rafe surprised him by joining in, picking the higher notes in harmony. Krissy had her hands braced on the ground and one leg in the air, but she popped her ear buds out and turned her head their way to listen.

They continued into the next verse, but Rafe stared at his phone the whole time, as if singing was something he just *did* without noticing or needing to concentrate. His breath control was impressive too, his voice softer than Mikey would've expected.

It sent a chill through Mikey, reminding him of that first time he'd sung with the choir—the notes playing off one another, voices intermingling to create a perfectly meshed melody. It also brought back memories of another time and place. Of singing with another man and losing himself to the music. To the inescapable, unrelenting feeling of wanting something he shouldn't.

It was a feeling that needed to go away. Now.

When they finished the piece, Rafe met his gaze. "Do you know what that song's about?" he asked quietly.

"Sure." Mikey always did his research before bringing a song to work. "The video had religious undertones, but Michael Stipe said it was about having a crush. About being boxed in by your feelings and worrying about putting yourself out there, telling the other person how you feel."

He cast a sideways glimpse toward Krissy. Despite her upside-down position, her shoulders crept up to her ears in flushed pleasure.

"Maybe that's what he told the press," Rafe said. "But Stipe is from Georgia. 'Losing your religion' is a southern expression about being pushed to the end of your rope. So far that it completely destroys your faith."

Across the room, Krissy's body went rigid. Everything got very quiet.

"I guess that's one interpretation," Mikey said.

Rafe stared at the ground, his brows drawn tightly together, lips pursed in a frown. "Yeah."

Then Rafe's phone rang. One look at his screen, and his demeanor completely shifted, that carefree smile returning as he picked up the call.

"Merrick!" Rafe sprang from his chair and sauntered toward the bedroom. "Yeah, I'm in town. You coming through for me tomorrow?" A pause was followed by laughter. "I meant with the tickets, you freak."

He closed the door behind him.

Mikey took a deep breath. Krissy had plugged her headphones in again, her body in a triangle and her palm reaching toward the ceiling. He didn't want to bother her with asking what Rafe meant by his comment, so he strummed through several more songs while she finished her routine. A light sheen of sweat was on her forehead when she rolled up her mat and plopped down next to him.

"You have a very pretty voice," she said.

Mikey felt his cheeks heat. He placed the guitar on the floor. "Thank you."

She curled her legs under her and cocked her head to the side. "I don't get it."

"Get what?"

"How the music and the landscaping jobs come together."

"Simple. The landscaping pays the bills. The music doesn't." It was an easier explanation than the truth.

"But you live with your folks. They don't charge you rent, do they?"

They didn't, only asking him to pay his share of the utilities, but that wasn't the reason he was still at home. Sure, he could've found a place to rent. Could've spent some of the cash he'd saved up on a used car instead of riding his bike everywhere. He would've liked to have said he had a plan, that he was saving money for something, but the reality was he hated being alone.

"No, but they wouldn't be so keen on me abandoning the business and still living there while I found something else. And I don't know if I want to. I like working in nature, when it doesn't beat up my hands, that is."

He tried to hide his hands between his knees, not wanting her to see how the winter weather had toughened skin already calloused from playing guitar, but Krissy's gaze dropped down to them anyway. With slow movements, she reached over and stroked the knuckles on his right hand.

Her gentle touch was soothing. Mikey eased his hand out from where it had been trapped and turned it over. Krissy paused and gazed at him with those wide eyes of hers, vivid purple framed by dark lashes. Her hand hovered over his in a move that asked for permission.

He nodded, too quickly. Too eagerly, but he didn't care. This felt natural with her. It felt *right*.

She traced a fingertip along his palm, one soft caress over his lifeline. It was chaste yet sensual at the same time, and each soft brush was a conversation they hadn't been able to have over the phone. It was like magic, the way they were talking without speaking, the way her touch seemed to wash away every impure thought he'd had. Her shirt had pulled to the side, revealing a tempting glimpse of her shoulder and neck, and he imagined lifting the fabric off her completely, feeling the warmth of her skin and the shape of her breasts.

She stroked each of his fingers from base to tip, and Mikey's pulse thrummed wildly. He wanted her stroking him elsewhere. Wanted that small, delicate hand wrapped around his cock, pumping and squeezing until he was groaning her name.

His sexual cravings were giving him whiplash, but he forced any other thought but her out of his head. This was what he'd prayed for, and he'd be damned if he wasn't going to take advantage of it. It was risky, letting things happen while Rafe was in the other room, but he'd been in there a while. It was possible the guy had fallen asleep.

Mikey touched her hand in return. He mapped out her hands like a blind man reading Braille, wanting to learn every line, every whorl. Krissy threaded her fingers through his and inched closer to him until their mouths finally met, lips coming together in the barest press of a kiss.

He inhaled deeply, wanting to take this slow, to make it last. Krissy, however, had other ideas. She kissed him again. Hard.

The aggressive move sent his heartbeat to full throttle. He barely had time to think before she put her hands on his chest, pushing him onto his back and climbing on top of him. Heat flooded through him as her legs caged his, her yoga pants so thin he could feel her warmth through his jeans. Eyes closed, he grasped her hips and held on. Krissy sucked on his lower lip and bit down, her lower body rolling with the movement. Mikey panted and arched up sharply. He was drowning in sensation, craving Krissy's bare body and the feeling of her touch, her mouth, of sliding inside her...until reality crept into his brain and cracked it open.

He hadn't told her about his virginal status yet.

It was presumptuous to assume they'd be having sex, but if she wanted to, then he'd have to tell her right before they went at it, which could ruin things. Or he could not tell her and risk coming in two seconds, which could *really* ruin things.

He chose the lesser of two evils and broke off the kiss. "Krissy, wait."

She sat up. "Did I do something wrong?"

"No...there's something I need to tell you."

"Okay." She was as short of breath as he was. Mikey released his grip on her hips and adjusted his glasses, smudged now from being mashed against his face during their kiss. He almost preferred the smear to the embarrassment of having to tell her this.

Damn him and his stupid need to be honest.

"I'm..." He cringed. Glanced up at her. "I'm a virgin."

FOUR

Oh God. Please, *please* don't let this have anything to do with the church job.

"Are you saving yourself for marriage or something?" Krissy asked.

Mikey huffed out a sound that could've resembled a laugh, if it didn't sound so sad. "I'd like to say that, 'cause it sounds better than the truth. Really I've just never had the opportunity."

"How is that possible? You're so cute."

The grim look on his face wavered slightly. "Thank you."

Krissy shook her head. The idea that no one had wanted him was preposterous. Chicks totally dug skinny guys. And he could sing too. That had to have made him at least a double threat in the dating world.

"Why didn't you tell me before?" she asked.

"I was worried you wouldn't understand."

"That's silly. Everyone's a virgin at some point," she said reassuringly. She nearly felt like one herself, considering how long it had been. But this complicated things. "You've done some...stuff though, right?"

"You want, like, a base or something?"

She giggled and tried not to be aware of his hard-on, still nestled between her thighs. "That would work."

"Third. Not in a while though."

"You haven't dated anyone?"

He shrugged. "I tried online dating, but it didn't work. I've had trouble...connecting with people." He glanced up at her, and his expression was an adorable mix of bashfulness and hope. "That changed when I met you."

Krissy grinned widely. She was hoping their connection was real and not a fleeting emotion she couldn't trust. Mikey's easygoing nature made her think he could be the calm in her storm. And his hands. *God*, his hands. Watching him play guitar had been like watching porn.

She'd always had a thing for hands, the intimacy of human touch. It was one of the reasons she'd been so amped up after that fake threesome scene. Rafe and the other guy's hands on her, even in ways suitable for a live audience, had been enough to get her blood pumping.

The other reason was her.

If anxiety and frequent mood shifts weren't fun enough, an out-of-control sex drive was one more feature of bipolar disorder. It was a symptom her meds had never managed to tamp down much and one she remembered having long before her hospital stint, to be honest, but the constant horniness was like wearing a heavy, freak-of-nature scarlet A around her neck, Flava Flav style.

Rafe had been the first person to tell her she didn't have to be defined by her illness. The first to build her a blanket fort, curl up in it with her, and stay there while she hid from the world.

She hadn't told Mikey it was Rafe she'd done the scene with. The way he'd reacted when she mentioned it at all made her gut plummet. Telling him how Rafe had picked up on her anxiety during her audition, taken her aside, and promised she was safe there would be easy. Saying she'd been immediately attracted to him and had talked with him afterward in his apartment for hours, confessing similar histories before falling asleep and waking up reaching for each other hours later? Not so much.

Confessing that to Mikey could ruin the shaky foundation of a relationship they'd built, but Rafe was right. She couldn't keep hiding the truth, not when he'd been honest with her.

She climbed off him and knelt by his side. Mikey sat up, frowning.

"Are you totally turned off to me now?" he asked.

"No," Krissy replied with a quick shake of her head. "But I have something to tell you too."

"Okay."

"You might've noticed some...unusual things about my routine."

"I did, but I didn't want to pry."

Her stomach did a somersault. God, he was sweet. With her heart pounding against her rib cage, she took a breath and began her practiced soliloquy.

"At the beginning of my sophomore year at NYU, I started having these periods of intense energy. I'd be awake till three in the morning, getting ahead in my assignments, walking the floors of my dorm practicing a monologue or a dance routine. I'd sleep two hours, go to class, and do it all again."

"Sounds like college."

"True, but it got worse, and these *things* kept happening. I'd be going to class and wind up at an art exhibit thirty blocks uptown. I had trouble remembering lines and song lyrics, but I thought I just needed to focus, you know? Buckle down. Work harder."

He nodded, and Krissy felt like she was breathing through a straw.

"Right before finals, I went to this stress-release party, and I kinda didn't stop when the party was over."

She couldn't make herself churn out the details. Forgetting to eat or drink before hanging out with people she barely knew. Getting high first on pot, then on little tablets someone handed her. Sex with a string of random guys whose names she couldn't remember. She woke up in dirty clothes with a stranger in her bed, humiliated and dehydrated and certain every student on campus was after her.

"I crashed at the end of it," she said. "Really bad. Like, couldn't-get-out-of-bed bad. By the time my roommate called health services and told them I hadn't left the room in days, I'd missed all my exams. I needed to be hospitalized."

"For exhaustion?" he asked. His eyes were such a lovely color. A soft, doe-eyed brown. She should memorize them now, so she could remember later how he used to look at her.

"No." Krissy swallowed, her mouth going dry. "For bipolar disorder."

She allowed the requisite beat for him to absorb that news, then moved on, talking as fast as she could.

"My parents checked me in at Yale-New Haven Psychiatric, which was great because, hey, if you're going to go crazy somewhere, you might as well do it where the Ivy League doctors are!"

Crap, she'd used the word-that-shall-not-be-named again. The humor didn't produce its desired effect either—nervous laughter that would cut through the discomfort, giving Mikey space to express his condolences while searching for a hasty exit. But he wasn't shrinking away in disgust. There was no judgment in his eyes, no revulsion evident in the little notches between his eyebrows. Just sadness.

"How long were you there?" he asked.

"Two weeks. The doctors stabilized me once they found the

right drugs. One gave me insomnia, another made my anxiety even worse, and the anti-depressant they had me on practically turned me into a zombie. Now I'm just on an anti-psychotic." She laughed. "Just."

As if that was no big deal at all. She kept talking.

"I started seeing a therapist when I got out, and my parents worked it so I got a medical leave of absence and was able to make up my exams. I took summer and January term classes to catch up, so I'll still be able to graduate on time." She shrugged and stepped into character, going fully into Healthy-Krissy-Mode. "It sucks, but it's something I have to deal with. I thought you should know, before we..."

She waved a hand between the two of them, implying whatever that implied.

Mikey's brows drew even more tightly together. Then his mouth dropped open in an expression that resembled...relief?

"*That's* why Rafe gave you a pill last night. He makes sure you get your medication."

So he had seen that. "I'm usually good with taking it, but I was totally wiped."

"And that's why your parents check in on you. To make sure you're okay."

"Pretty much, but I've been stable for a while now. I take my meds, track my moods, get the right amount of sleep, and do my daily yoga practice. As long as I avoid any—" she made air quotes with her fingers, "—*triggering* behaviors, I live like any other normal college student."

Sure she did. That was why she'd asked her parents to let her move in with Rafe, too embarrassed to go back to her dorm and face the former roommate who ducked corners every time Krissy saw her around campus. Too worried about the drugs and partying that were readily available. Too scared to be in an actual relationship, so she messed around with her hetero-flexible best friend instead.

"Why didn't you tell me this before?" he asked.

Krissy ducked her head, peeking up at him. "I was afraid you wouldn't understand."

He smiled softly at the repetition of his words. She was about to drop the next bombshell when Mikey lifted a hand and caressed her cheek.

"You're so brave," he said.

"I am?"

"Yes. I can't imagine how hard it must've been for you to tell me that." He brushed a thumb over her skin, so lightly she shivered. "Thank you for confiding in me."

Shock stole her voice. She'd expected revulsion or fear from him, or worse, the same looks of sympathetic pity she got from her family. She hadn't expected him to *thank* her.

"You're welcome," she whispered.

He went serious, the movement of his thumb ceasing as his gaze dropped to her lips. He cupped her cheek and urged her toward him, the slow, romantic moves like something out of a movie. Her pulse was flying so fast she could hardly breathe when he kissed her.

Krissy let him take the lead, keeping still in a desperate effort to hold back the torrent of desire inside her. Mikey took his time, as if kissing wasn't something he did often and didn't want to rush. She swore he trembled when he kissed her again, wet passes of his lower lip followed by a quick swipe of tongue.

The taste of him was gasoline to her fire.

"Touch me. Please, Mikey."

He swallowed. "Where?"

She answered by dragging his hand toward her waistline. Mikey groaned, then looked over her shoulder and grabbed the blanket, tugging it over them.

They stretched out side by side, and Krissy snuggled closer, wanting his warmth, his acceptance. She knew she had more to tell him—she wasn't done coming clean yet—but not now. Not when he was kissing her again and his fingers were inching under the waistband of her leggings. Sliding into her panties and making a rough circle over her clit.

"Oh, *fuck.*"

Mikey's touch halted. "Sorry, my fingers are calloused."

"No," she gasped. "They're perfect."

His slightly heavy-handed touch was nothing like Rafe's confident caress, but something about the combination of his coarse skin and uncertainty, how gently he was handling her and the sweet, innocent look in his eyes, revved her up like a packed house on opening night. And she'd forgotten what it was like, to be kissed and touched by someone who might have actual feelings for her.

"More," she begged him. "Please."

He rubbed her again, touch halting and quickening as he offered her clumsy kisses. It felt so good, but she wanted to be pleasing him at the same time. Wanted to feel him in her hand and watch him shudder from her touch.

She reached for his belt. "Can I?"

"Yeah. God, yeah." Mikey's circles grew uneven as he struggled to undo his pants with his other hand. Krissy reached in to do the job for him, fumbling with his clothes until she'd wrapped her fingers around the thick length of him.

His mouth dropped open, touch slowing to a near stop. "Krissy." Her name came out more as a moan than a word.

She arched her hips and whimpered, a plea for him to keep going while she slowly pumped. He complied, albeit unsteadily, and their bodies grew sweaty under the blanket, hot breath mixing and fogging up Mikey's glasses. He got her so close she was hovering near the edge, but her orgasm was just out of reach, and for a second she missed Rafe—the way he knew her responses, how easily he picked up her cues to go faster, harder, *now*. Closing her eyes, she imagined him behind her, his long, thin fingers with perfectly buffed nails working in tandem with Mikey's. Sliding inside her, the two of them making her come together.

It was the fantasy he'd coaxed from her the last time he'd had his hand worked into her panties.

It sent her over the edge.

She clutched Mikey's shirt with her free hand and pressed her face against his chest to muffle her cries. As soon as the pleasure abated, guilt sliced, sharp and deep. She shouldn't have been thinking about Rafe. Not while Mikey was looking at her like this, as if her orgasm was the most beautiful thing he'd ever seen.

"Good?" he asked, but the slight turn of his lips showed a glimmer of confidence.

"Very. Now it's your turn."

His cock kicked in her grip. Krissy pulled her hand away long enough to lick her palm, then rode her slickened fist down over him. Mikey's breath rushed out, eyes drifting closed.

"Please," he begged, the strain in his voice showing his desperation. "Please do it. Please make me come."

"That's the idea."

He choked out a laugh, then pinched his eyes shut. Krissy watched his face as she worked him, enjoying his responses and the decadent mix of satin and steel under her caress. His breath caught when she sped up, and his expression of anguished pleasure had her greedily waiting for his release when the bedroom door swung open.

"Okay kids," Rafe's voice boomed out. "I'm going to bed."

Krissy stopped moving, her hand frozen around Mikey's cock.

He didn't move either, eyes mashed shut, his entire body as rigid as the still-pulsing flesh in her hand.

"Oooh, did I interrupt something?" Rafe asked. "My bad."

"Not interrupting anything, except us falling asleep," Krissy insisted around a fake yawn. Her theatrical skills might need polishing, but they were decent enough to make her sound legit. Besides, the blanket hid what they were doing.

Rafe crossed his arms and leaned back against the wall. "You two need to get it on already. The sexual tension in here is practically giving *me* a hard-on."

Mikey strangled a grunt. The sound was coupled with another twitch of his cock and the slightest kick of his hips.

Wait a minute. Was the idea of Rafe getting hard turning him on? Was that why he'd never...

No. No way. That particular fantasy was too off the wall to think about.

"Well I'm gonna crash," Rafe said. "We've got tickets for the matinee tomorrow, so I'll see you lovebirds in the morning."

"Night," Krissy called out casually. When Rafe had closed the bedroom door behind him, she glanced at Mikey. "Do you want to keep going?"

He shook his head. "Mood's a bit broken, you know?"

Nudging her hand away, Mikey tucked himself back in his jeans. He was still hard though, the denim bulging after he'd zippered. Disappointment lodged like a stone in her gut.

"Sorry," she said. "I guess I owe you one."

He made a noise, a tense sound that came from the back of his throat. He wouldn't make eye contact, and Krissy's nerves crept back in—voices in her head whispering that he didn't actually want to be with her, that he'd only said what he did in the hopes that she'd get him off. After all, no one in their right mind would want to take on somebody who was mentally ill.

Then Mikey touched her hand, a light brush of his fingertips along hers.

"It's okay. And I meant what I said before. Thank you for telling me." She still had the sense that he was managing the situation until their eyes met. The dimples on either side of his mouth appeared when he smiled. "I'm gonna wash up, okay?"

She nodded, her anxieties rushing out like the tide. Nothing was wrong here, other than an unfortunate interruption. Mikey swung his legs over the side of the futon and went into the bathroom. Krissy tiptoed toward the bedroom, finding her pjs in a neat pile by the door, phone charger and pill bottle on top of it.

Rafe.

Warmth filled her chest even as sadness rushed in beside it. It had hurt when he'd admitted he could never be with her in the long run after that first heavy make-out-and-petting session, because she'd thought he was perfect for her in so many ways. But she'd accepted that his heart didn't work that way.

A part of her had actually been a little relieved.

They both knew she wasn't ready for a relationship, and being friends with benefits was the best of both worlds. Now she finally was doing what he'd encouraged—taking a stab at a chance to be with someone who could give her everything. And for the first time in so long, that felt possible.

Padding into the kitchen area, Krissy filled a cup with water and downed her pill. Outside the windows, downtown Portland glittered in the distance, its lights mirrored on the black surface of the water. Calming, like Mikey's presence.

Thumbing across her phone screen, Krissy opened her mood journal app and grinned at the happy emoticon waiting there.

You haven't logged your mood yet. How are you feeling right now?

Great. She was feeling great.

FIVE

The next afternoon, Krissy and Rafe sat in the living room while Mikey took his turn in the bathroom. They'd spent the morning watching a Harry Potter marathon after making another massive breakfast, this one with the addition of home fries and bacon. Rafe had teased her as soon as Mikey hit the shower, apologizing for ruining their fun the night before.

"Nothing happened," she insisted.

Rafe rolled his eyes. "Nothing, my ass. He's cute. I'd even call him hot, if we could upgrade that haircut from geek to geek-chic somehow. And he obviously likes you. So what's the hold-up?"

Krissy let her silence answer for her, focusing on tying her laces instead.

She'd paired her high-topped Chucks with a long-sleeved flannel shirt and bright-green leggings, her hair in pigtails. The hairstyle was more a necessity than a fashion statement. She'd felt more confident about her updated look after Mikey's compliment —the pop of color from her contacts and her bleached strands made her feel like she was seeing a different person every time she looked in the mirror—but the static electricity in the air was making her new layers frizz out like a lion's mane.

"Is it because of us?" Rafe asked. Krissy nodded. "You don't *have* to tell him. But it's good to start things off by being honest."

Krissy cringed. She did have to tell Mikey, but...ugh.

"There isn't a guidebook on how to have that conversation with a prospective boyfriend, Rafe, even if he took the news of my being crazy well."

"Kris..." he warned.

She huffed out a sigh. "Of my *having an illness* well."

The look of pride on his face at her reply dissolved quickly into a smirk. Rafe unguarded was a fleeting thing, like a comet or a shooting star. He folded his hands behind his head and stretched his long legs out in front of him.

"If it helps, I'd be willing to facilitate things. Make it a real-life version of what we did on stage."

Now it was her turn to roll her eyes. *"That's* crazy."

"Why?" he asked with a smug grin. "You said you wanted it. Think of it as a belated Chanukah present."

"That's like the most fucked-up present ever."

He winked, and damn if the idea of her wildest fantasy coming true didn't make her stomach jolt with excitement. But there was no way that was happening.

Hey Mikey, I really like you, but I also have this thing going on with my roommate. He's mostly into dudes though, so how about we all fuck and then talk it out in the morning?

Sure. Great idea.

A short time later, they were filing into the small theater in the Old Port. Krissy sat between Mikey and Rafe, her knee bobbing as she flipped through the playbill.

"I've always thought there's something incredible about the moments right before a show starts," she told Mikey. "The energy of the musicians tuning their instruments, the crowd just waiting to be dazzled."

And this show was going to be especially dazzling. It was a performance of the musical *Hair*, and a note in the program said the cast would be interacting with the audience, not to mention the partial nudity. But that part wasn't half as exciting to Krissy as the opportunity to watch people singing their hearts out. It always made the torch she carried for a life in the theater burn a little brighter.

"I never got to see the revival when it was on Broadway," she continued, her feet tapping a rhythm against the floor. "But I've practically memorized the soundtrack. I'm stoked I get to see it here."

She was talking too fast, and the chair was bouncing with her movements, but she didn't care. Mikey knew more about her now. She could be herself.

"You've always wanted to act?" he asked.

"Since I was a kid and my parents took me and my sister to see *Les Misérables*. I knew by intermission it was what I wanted to do with my life."

And they had supported her. They'd gotten her a vocal coach and come to every silly high school show she'd been in, waited for her outside during her audition for Tisch and applauded when the acceptance letter came.

Now all they did was ask her if she wanted to do something "less stressful", acting as if she were a china doll about to crack.

The house lights dimmed, the overture beginning, and Krissy wove her fingers tightly together as the cast traipsed in from the wings. Rafe's friend Merrick was starring in the role of George Berger, and once he'd sauntered onto the stage, he leapt off it and into the audience. He immediately climbed onto the armrests of Rafe's chair and pretended to grind against her roommate's face.

Oh, yeah. This was going to rock.

They launched into the opening number, and Krissy mouthed along to the lyrics. As the show progressed, the hum inside her got louder. The desire to be on the stage, the feeling of *I want to do that too.*

She could. She could dazzle the shit out of this audience. The stage-fright thing was BS.

She'd told Rafe her anxiety was because she didn't think she had a good voice. The fabrication was easier than admitting her fear of getting sick again, and what it could do to her career.

The worry had slithered into her thoughts during every audition the last two semesters, her voice cracking as she tried to reach notes she had no problem with in the shower. It only added to her parents' concerns that the long rehearsals, erratic schedules, the possibility of rejection, and periods of unemployment could trigger another episode.

But Krissy wasn't going to let that happen. Her strict routine ensured she was staying on top of things. She understood her illness wasn't some cold she was going to get over. This was forever. And the only way to avoid a repeat performance of her last hospitalization was to keep up with her studies, do what her shrink told her to do, and assure her family everything was fine.

The title song started, and Krissy let herself fall into it, forgetting everything else and dancing in her seat. Midway through the number, Merrick pulled a rolled-up piece of paper from his pocket and lit it up in the middle of the stage.

It was a prop, a fake joint lined in powder, but it edged the memories under her skin nonetheless. Suddenly, she was inundated by them—the awful things she'd done the last time she got high. The bad choices and wild, inappropriate behavior. The vast wasteland of depression she'd fallen into after she'd lost her grip on reality.

She grasped the armrests, trying to stay calm.

Nothing is happening to me. I'm in control.

Rafe's mouth was at her ear a second later. "Should we leave?"

"No," she whispered back. He and Mikey should at least be able to enjoy the show. She'd take a breather. Do a lotus pose on a bench she'd seen. "You guys stay. I'll chill in the lobby." She gathered her coat from under the seat and turned to Mikey. "I'm gonna sit the rest of this act out."

"Are you okay?"

"Just need some air. I'll see you guys at intermission."

"I'll go with you."

"No, you stay and watch. I'll have to field a call from my mom and dad anyway."

She made her way quickly up the aisle before he could stop her or ask more questions. Chalk one up for her parents—no way could she make a career out of acting if some fake smoke gave her an anxiety attack in the middle of a performance.

She pushed the door open and tiptoed out of the theater.

* * *

MIKEY WATCHED KRISSY LEAVE, bewildered by her sudden departure. A sickening heaviness settled in his stomach as he turned back around in his seat. He was out of his element here. He'd done a quick search about bipolar disorder on his phone when she was in the shower this morning, but Wikipedia didn't help other than to give him a clinical overview. She'd said she had to avoid any triggers, but he couldn't figure out what set her off.

Letting her leave didn't seem right—she'd been so excited to see this, and now she was sitting in the lobby alone—but Mikey didn't know what to do.

Rafe would, though.

He'd kept his interactions with Krissy's roommate to a

minimum today, but there was no avoiding the guy now. Not if he could shed some light on what was going on with Krissy. Leaning over the empty seat between them, Mikey whispered, "Should one of us go after her?"

Rafe shook his head. "She'll get embarrassed if we make a big deal out of it. Best to let her be. Intermission is soon anyway."

Mikey nodded and slumped back into his chair, trying to concentrate on the show as the actors sang about life and love, about rebelling against their conservative parents and society. About being free to be whoever they wanted with no guilt.

Do whatever he wanted, as long as he didn't hurt anyone? Sure. He'd get right on that. As soon as he stopped thinking about how corrupt it was to have gotten even harder last night when Rafe walked in on him and Krissy. How he'd stolen away from her like the couch was on fire and jerked off in the bathroom to the idea of Rafe giving him instructions on the best ways to fuck her. To the thought of Krissy sucking them both off. Rafe's cock in his mouth while Krissy watched. Him watching her and Rafe coming together.

Wrong. So fucking wrong. And so much worse than anything he'd fantasized about before. Apparently the fact that he'd wanted a man once in his life wasn't enough. Now he needed to add orgy to the list of things he had to banish from his thoughts.

At least before it had been only one person at a time—one guy he'd wanted before he'd escaped college and lived the life of a monk. Now he was attracted to both Krissy and Rafe. It was a violation of everything he'd been taught, deviation in its worst form.

Maybe it was because of what she'd told him about that show she'd been in, his lizard brain taking her theatrical experience and turning it into another messed-up fantasy. He'd looked up the Theory of Deviance this morning too. It was described as an absence of conformity; any thought, feeling, or action that violated social laws.

Well, he was just the freaking poster child for that, wasn't he? He was going to need about a year of confession to cleanse himself of these thoughts.

But that was all they were—thoughts. He wasn't hurting anyone by thinking, so maybe these people on the stage who saw their sexuality as gifts, and not as something dirty, were right.

People onstage who were now naked.

It was only for a second. They'd hidden themselves under a giant parachute and resurfaced completely nude right before the room went black. The house lights came on a few seconds later, the stage totally empty. Mikey blinked when the announcement for intermission came over the speakers and people started moving out of their seats.

"You all right over there?"

Mikey glanced at Rafe. The actors' nude bodies were still imprinted on his brain, a flash that remained on your retina long after the picture was taken.

"Sure. Why?"

Rafe dropped his head back against the seat and laughed, then shook his head. Mikey's gut sank like lead in water. There was a knowing glimmer in the other man's velvet gaze, as if he could read every thought Mikey had.

"This show is a bust." Rafe put on his coat and stood. "Let's get out of here."

"Shouldn't we check with Krissy first?" It felt weird, making this decision without her.

"If she was stressed enough to leave, she's not going to want to come back in. And you look halfway scandalized."

"I'm not scandalized," Mikey replied defensively. "Just surprised. That was a whole lotta naked up there."

Rafe snorted. His teeth gleamed, pearlescent. "Come on.

Krissy will be happier at the apartment with you anyway. You go find her. I'll tell Merrick we're heading out."

They went in different directions, Rafe hopping onto the stage and walking confidently behind the curtain as if he belonged there, Mikey toward the back of the house. He found Krissy in the lobby sitting cross-legged on a bench against the wall. She looked so sad, so lost and nervous, rolling and unrolling the hem of her shirt. Her eyes lit up when she saw him.

"Hey." She hopped up and bounded toward him. "Sorry I had to run out, but I'm fine now, I promise. Where's Rafe?"

"He went to tell Merrick we're leaving."

Her face fell. "Because of me?"

Watching the happiness drain out of her was like a knife plunging into his chest. "Nah. I wasn't really enjoying the show either."

"You weren't?" she asked, hope lighting up her eyes.

"Yeah, too much nudity."

A small smile formed on her face. "You have a problem with nudity?"

Her grin grew impish, a playful gleam emerging from beneath her thick, dark lashes that Mikey wanted to use as a cloak. A shield against all his impure thoughts.

"Not where you're concerned." The line was ridiculously cheesy, but she giggled anyway. Thank goodness. "You sure you're okay, though? I didn't know what bothered you in there, and I'd like to stop it from happening again, if I can."

She went up and down on her toes a few times, pensive. "The fake pot smoke reminded me of stuff that happened when I was sick. I know it wasn't real, but it took me back there."

"Okay. No smoke of any kind. Got it." He gave a firm nod, glad to have something solid to work with. "I guess we'll go back to the apartment then?"

"Unless you wanted to do something else?"

He'd had other tour destinations in mind, but most of them required daylight, and the sun was already kissing the horizon. "Let's grab a pizza and chill. It's only Sunday. We have the rest of the week to see the town."

Her smile returned to full-Krissy-wattage, and Mikey's heart felt like the Grinch's at the end of the movie, growing two sizes larger until he thought it would burst.

Rafe returned a few moments later. "I told Merrick you weren't feeling well. He said he was sorry and offered us all a complimentary backstage tour tomorrow."

"Aces!" Krissy said with a fist pump. "Let's jet, fellas."

She turned on her heel and skipped to the door.

They stopped for a few slices at a place with a view over the docks, then went back to the apartment. Mikey stood awkwardly in the living room, trying not to ogle them as they took their coats off. Krissy in her leggings that showed off every curve. Rafe looking like a male model in a turtleneck and dark-washed jeans.

Christ, what was the matter with him? He'd spent the last two days worrying they were a couple, and now that he was pretty sure Krissy wanted him, all he could do was crave them both. Was this his subconscious's way of ensuring he'd be a virgin forever?

The two of them exchanged glances, a silent connection that put Mikey's suspicions back on high alert. Rafe turned toward him, his lips turned up in a slow grin.

"I have an idea," he said. "Let's play a game."

SIX

"What kind of game?" Krissy asked warily. The look on Rafe's face wasn't to be trusted.

"A board game, silly. I haven't played one in forever." He walked over to the collection by the TV and knelt down, picking through them until he found a box he liked. "Let's play Sorry, the game of sweet revenge."

"You *would* choose that," Krissy chided. She wasn't sure what Rafe's motives were. Playing a game seemed to go against his desire for her to tell Mikey the truth, but she'd take it if it meant she could stall the inevitable a little longer.

As Rafe sat on the futon and began unpacking game pieces, Krissy turned to Mikey and asked quietly, "This okay?"

"Sure. Whatever you want."

Her heart leapt. No, pirouetted was more like it. She'd felt so stupid for having a meltdown in the theater, but Mikey hadn't blinked an eye, simply asking what he could do to make it better.

"Awesome, I'm just gonna grab my meds."

She ran to the bedroom and downed her pill, then sprinted back to the couch. Mikey and Rafe were on opposite sides of the futon. She shimmied in between them and sat down. Her knee pressed against Mikey's and stayed there.

"I say we make this interesting," Rafe said. "Usual rules, except when you bump someone's pawn back to start, you get to ask that person a question. Same if you land on a slide that's not your own color."

"What types of questions are we asking?" she asked.

"Any kind you want." The southern drawl Rafe tried so hard to hide slipped out on the letter *i*. He shuffled the cards. "Everybody choose your pawns."

She chose blue while Mikey picked green and Rafe decided on red. They each drew cards and made moves. Krissy was the first to bump Rafe back to home.

She did a little victory dance in her seat. "How old are you?"

He rolled his eyes. "You know the answer to that."

"Yeah, but Mikey doesn't."

Another eye roll was coupled with a shake of Rafe's head. "I'm twenty-seven." He chucked a card at Krissy. "Make your next question less boring."

They each drew cards again, and Krissy groaned when Rafe sent her pawn to the starting point.

"What was the first thing you said to me when you got back from your visit here?" he asked.

She squeezed her eyes shut. "I hate you."

"That's not what you said."

"I said I loved Maine."

"Liar, liar, pants on fire," Rafe sang.

She opened her eyes, grabbed a yellow pawn from the box, and threw it at him. He laughed and caught it. "Come on, Krissy. You can't lie during the game of Sorry."

"Otherwise known as The Game That Screws Krissy Over." She turned to face Mikey and sighed. "I told him I thought I'd finally found someone who got me."

Mikey bumped her shoulder with his. "So did I."

A thrill went through her, bringing back the memory of his mouth on hers. On her next turn, Krissy was able to skid her pawn along a green slide. She shifted Mikey's way and leaned close enough to whisper, "Did you want to kiss me yesterday in the truck?"

"Yeah," he whispered back.

"Hey!" Rafe hollered. "No keeping secrets during Sorry."

Mikey pinched his lips together, amusement in his eyes. "Sorry, not sorry."

The two men exchanged friendly looks, seeming for the first time like they felt comfortable around each other. It made Krissy's body hum with an energy better than any drug. She reached for a card, cheering when she saw the word *Sorry* printed across it, and knocked one of Rafe's pawns back home.

He stared at her. "It was *my* turn, Krissy."

Her shoulders lifted with her giggle. "Oops."

They continued playing, chasing each other around the game board. All but one of Krissy's pawns had made it to safety when Rafe pulled a card that let him skate across a blue slide. He sat back and pursed his lips while she waited for her question.

"What's your favorite sex act?" he asked.

She narrowed her eyes at him, her cheeks going hot. "Can I veto this question?"

Rafe chuckled. "No."

She glared at him, but what the hell? This wasn't the worst thing she had to admit by far. "Being fingered. I'm boring, I guess."

Mikey cleared his throat, then shifted so his knee nudged hers. "You couldn't be boring if you tried."

The small touch made her shiver, the compliment making her face flare even hotter.

"Awww," Rafe said. "You guys are so cute."

He nudged her other knee, prodding her closer to Mikey, and the double points of contact made her skin tingle. The fantasy that had driven her over the edge last night came flooding back, and Krissy had to clench her hands into fists to stave off the torrent of images, old ones and new: Them touching her. Her touching them.

Them touching each other.

Her next move gave her a chance to ask Mikey another question, but she couldn't think clearly. "Can I pass?"

"No way," Rafe said. "We'll default to a version of the last inquiry." His grin was pure evil when he turned to Mikey. "So, Mr. Pelletier. What's your favorite sexual position?"

Shit. "You don't have to answer that," Krissy assured him.

"Yeah he does. Rules are rules."

The look Krissy threw Rafe's way clearly said *shut up*, but he wasn't backing down.

"Come on, Mikey. Fess up. Krissy won't care if it's dirty. But remember, you've gotta tell the truth."

Mikey's voice was low when he said, "I don't have a favorite, because I haven't done it."

It wasn't often that Rafe was stunned into silence, but that did the trick.

"Oh...damn." He let out a nervous laugh. "Sorry, Mikey. Didn't mean to put you on the spot there."

Mikey didn't answer. Krissy turned the tables on her roommate.

"What about you?" she asked, arms crossed in a challenge. She knew Rafe's sensitive spots, but since actual intercourse was sexuala-non-grata, this was information that had eluded her.

"I'm not the one who lost their turn," he said. "You don't get to ask me a question."

"Don't care. Answer it anyway."

He smiled broadly, then conceded. "It depends on who I'm

with. With girls I like to be on top. With guys, I prefer bottoming."

"Wait, so you're..." Mikey started, his eyes wide.

"Bi." Rafe's verification came out so matter-of-factly, typical of an actor who was confident in his sexuality and his looks. It was not typical, however, of someone who'd been through what he had. "Krissy didn't tell you?"

"No," Mikey replied stiffly, and Krissy reached for her pawns. Rafe's intentions with the game were finally clear. He was going to use it to worm out the truth and broadcast it like a billboard in Times Square.

"This is a dumb game," she said. "Let's play something else."

Rafe threw an arm out to stop her. "You're just saying that because you're losing."

He reached for a card, and his move bumped her last piece backward. He flicked the card a few times before dropping it in the pile.

"What was that fantasy you told me about? The one involving Mikey."

Even with only their knees touching, Krissy felt Mikey go rigid. She was pretty sure he could feel the same from her.

"You know the answer to that," she said, but there wasn't the same mirth in her tone as there had been when Rafe had said it.

"Mikey doesn't."

Krissy crossed her arms. Stared up at the ceiling, then at her lap. She wanted to lie, desperate to cover up the truth, but there was that burning, hungry part of her that didn't want to hide, and Rafe probably wouldn't let her anyway.

"Having a threesome," she admitted quietly. "With both of you."

Rafe sat back on the couch and slinked an arm around her. "What do you say, Mikey? Want to help me make Krissy's fantasy a reality?"

Oh God. Rafe was doing this. He was actually doing this. Krissy braced herself for Mikey's response, waiting for him to completely freak out, the endgame she'd expected all along when he found out the truth.

"Help you?" he sputtered.

"Sure." Rafe twirled one of her pigtails around his finger. "You two obviously don't know how to get things started on your own, and I'm getting bored watching. Someone needs to get the ball rolling."

Mikey's mouth dropped open. There was so much insecurity in his eyes. "So, you two are together."

"No," she said quickly. "Not in the way you think."

"What *way*, then?"

Krissy couldn't speak, couldn't figure out any way to tell him that didn't sound one hundred percent certifiably nuts.

Please don't think I'm crazy.

"We have a sexual relationship," Rafe answered for her, "but are strictly platonic otherwise."

It hurt to hear him say it out loud, but not as much as the look on Mikey's face as his gaze darted between them. "I don't understand."

"We're not sleeping together," Krissy said. "We just...fool around."

His silence dragged on for several seconds. Or years. Krissy twisted her shirt in her hands and gave Mikey an imploring look, hoping he could see the apology in her eyes.

"Then you're not a couple," he finally said.

"Nope," Rafe confirmed, then winked at Mikey. "I sway a little more the other way."

Mikey exhaled in what could've been a laugh but wasn't, not really, and pushed his hair out of his eyes. Krissy found the courage to brush her fingers against his. By some miracle, he didn't wrench away.

"I'm sorry I didn't tell you. I didn't know how."

"And you still..." Mikey made a tentative sweep of his pinky along hers. "Want me?"

"Oh, she wants you, all right," Rafe interjected. "She's got a dirty little mind, this one. You should hear the stuff she's thought of about you." He shifted her on the couch until she faced Mikey and hooked his chin over her shoulder, positioning her like an offering. "So what do you say? Interested?"

Krissy's heart was pounding. Mikey swallowed, looked hard at her, and whispered, "You want this?"

She wanted to forge something real with Mikey. To trust him with her mind, body, and heart. But right now a haze of lust was clouding her mind, and all she wanted was to be sandwiched between them, a helpless prisoner while they did all sorts of delicious things to her, then to see if she had the skills to please them both at once.

"Yes," she answered. "I want this."

Another swallow. He nodded at her, then at Rafe. "Okay."

Krissy felt the shape of Rafe's smile, his breath hot on her cheek. "It's your show now, sweetheart. What do you want to do?"

She arched against him, then reached for Mikey, tangling their fingers together.

"Bedroom," she managed, her body alive with the need to kiss and touch and come, to act out the real-life version of what she'd only played at onstage. "I want you both in the bedroom."

Rafe coaxed her forward, and Krissy's legs were wobbly when she stood. He took her free hand, linking the three of them together, and she allowed herself to be towed down the hallway, Rafe in the lead, Mikey following closely behind her.

Inside the bedroom, Rafe let go of her, flicked on the bedside lamp, and reached for his belt. Krissy's breathing hitched at the tinny sound of metal unlatching. She watched him shuck his jeans, his powerful arms crossing his body as he dragged off his shirt. Hairless chest. Washboard abs. He really was one of God's most beautiful creations.

"You've seen all this before," Rafe teased. "Turn around and show Mikey what you want."

She moved slowly. Mikey's forehead was creased, his posture tense despite his quickened breaths. Krissy touched his glasses.

"Can I? You'll be able to see?"

He nodded. "I can see enough."

She slid the glasses off his face and placed them on the nightstand, then danced her touch at the hem of his sweater. He paused, then took her hands in his and slipped them under his shirt.

Oh, the relief. The delight over his acceptance. She felt like she was flying, and it juiced up her libido to epic proportions.

She hauled Mikey's sweater over his head, giving in to the desire, pure adrenaline taking over. His body was thin but paneled with flat, strong muscle. A trail of dark hair made a path from his navel to his waistline. She wove their fingers together and leaned in to kiss him, dipping her tongue into his mouth. He yielded to her, moaning softly as his tongue touched hers. It was a sound Krissy echoed when Rafe's hands skated around her waist and found the front of her shirt.

One by one, he popped the buttons open, then slid it off her shoulders before unhooking her bra. He dragged the straps down her arms, and Krissy broke the kiss, too turned on to breathe. Rafe dropped her bra to the floor and moved in behind her. He ran his knuckles along the sides of her breasts, slow up-and-down caresses that made her skin rise with gooseflesh, made her nipples bead up and tighten. She shivered and fell back against him.

"She's beautiful, isn't she?" he asked Mikey.

"Incredibly," he whispered.

Krissy could barely contain her shudder. Mikey ran a

fingertip along the underside of one breast, then circled her nipple. With his head cocked to the side, he pinched, and Krissy's responding gasp made him back off.

"No." She shook her head. "Don't stop."

He did it again. Repeated the action with the other nipple. Every tweak made her jolt, but Rafe palmed her hips, holding her still. A determined crease formed between Mikey's brows. He lowered his head and sucked one pert nub at a time, fondling the other when it was exposed to the air.

"Fuck," Krissy said on a surprised and pleased laugh. Mikey might have been a virgin, but he sure seemed to know what he was doing right now.

She reached back for Rafe, a frantic move that said *touch me, please*, but her roommate had other ideas. Kneeling behind her, he untied her laces, then urged her out of her shoes one at a time. He tugged down her leggings, helping her step out of them as Mikey continued to tease and torment her breasts. Once both her feet were on the ground again, Rafe trailed his touch up one of her legs until his fingers rode along her damp panties. He cupped her pussy, rocking her with steady pressure from the heel of his palm.

"Oh God." Krissy's knees nearly gave out. She clutched Mikey's arms in an attempt to stay upright. "Bed. Please. I can't..."

Her sentence died on a grunt when Rafe gave her another firm press. He chuckled at her reaction, then stood and climbed onto the bed.

Still keeping her grip on Mikey, she looked up at him. Despite the erection pressing at his slacks, she was still waiting for him to have second thoughts and book it out of here. But all he did was walk her backward toward the bed, surprising the hell out of her when he unzipped his pants, yanked them down, and kicked them off.

Fuck. Yes.

She stretched out on the bed next to Rafe. He feathered his touch over her hip, then leaned in to rake his teeth along her neck. His beard and mustache rasped over her skin, a tickling scrape that sensitized every nerve. Mikey lay down beside her with an awkward glance at Rafe, then zeroed in on her mouth.

Moving instinctively out of the way, Rafe bent his head lower and began suckling her breast. Krissy whimpered at the wet suction, but the sound got lost when Mikey kissed her again— hard and hungry, his mouth devouring hers. Rafe's fingers spanned her pelvis, sliding lower until they dipped into her panties. Krissy's breath rushed out when he parted her lips and traced a slippery circle over her clit.

She let out a moan, and Mikey pulled back, gaze dropping to where her roommate's hand moved beneath the fabric.

"Holy shit," he breathed.

"She's crazy wet," Rafe said, kissing her cheek. "She never gets like this with me. Must be you, Mikey."

It was embarrassing, having Rafe talk about her like that, but he was right. She could feel how slick she was—the result of being unbearably, startlingly turned on.

With an audible swallow, Mikey reached over and cautiously lifted the waistband of her panties. His nostrils flared, his tongue coming out to moisten his upper lip.

He liked to watch. Fucking *hell*, he liked to watch.

Discovering this little kink of his was almost too hot to handle. His eyes trained on Rafe's hand, Mikey ground his brief-clad erection against her hip. The fabric was damp where they touched, and Krissy felt the first trembling pulses of her release. She bucked up into Rafe's hand, and he read her signals, shifting the circles he was drawing to a pattern of quick up-and-down motions. She arched, seconds away from bliss when he stopped.

"No," she whined. She'd die if he left her on the edge like this, but Rafe simply smirked.

"Such a greedy little monster you are."

He worked her panties down her legs, and Mikey's hand drifted to her belly. Rafe hooked one of his strong thighs around hers and made a V over her clit with his pointer and middle fingers, spreading her open.

"What do you want, Krissy?"

She moaned again and squirmed between them, her hips lifting, body so empty she could cry. "Both of you," she replied breathlessly. "I want both your hands on me. Making me come."

He rocked his fingers back and forth. "And what do we get out of it?"

Death by pleasure. There had to be a special spot in hell for suffering like this. "I'll repay the favor."

Mikey's eyes met hers. Desire flashed in them.

Rafe lowered his fingers, circling her opening, a tease that sent tremors everywhere. "What do you think, Mikey? Should we take pity on her?"

Mikey's expression went a little devilish, a glance down her body coupled with a slow pass of his tongue along his upper lip.

"Yeah. Let's make that fantasy of hers come true."

"God." Krissy gripped the pillows. She'd never have guessed this sweet, beautiful virgin would be into one of her dirtiest wishes, and it was like the answer to her prayers.

"I like the way you think." Rafe leaned down and breathed hot in her ear. "Come for us, Krissy."

He plunged a finger inside her in a slow spiral, then dragged it out again, wrist twisting until he found the spot that made her thrash. Mikey skimmed his palm lower, and Krissy lifted her head to watch. It was the climax to a scene she'd imagined over and over again, and she cried out when he found her slit.

"Fuck, fuck, fuck."

Her head fell back against the pillow. Mikey's touch was more confident than it had been last night, two fingers rubbing hard and fast. Rafe began a slick pounding, and the dual sensations drove her back to the edge. She tried to hold on, tried to make it last, but one, two, three seconds later, her release bolted through her. She let go of the pillow to grip both their arms, her body jerking off the bed. When they'd wrung every drop of pleasure from her, she collapsed and tried to catch her breath.

Mikey's soft laugh was the first thing she heard. "Okay, that was ridiculously hot."

The sound was a glass of cold water on a humid day. She exhaled, and the tension seeped from her. Krissy rolled to face Mikey and nuzzled his cheek.

"Thank you," she whispered.

He was flushed, his hair in his eyes, and his grin slightly crooked, dimples showing.

"You're welcome." Mikey leaned in and pecked her on the lips. He gazed down at her, something blooming between them that didn't appear to need words or explanations.

She knew she owed him them, anyway.

Rafe tugged on one of her pigtails. "I can think of better ways for you to thank us than with words."

A glance back at him showed one quirked eyebrow. Even though she'd come only moments before, desire dashed through her belly, hot and insistent. She lifted a finger to outline the slender planes of Mikey's chest.

"Would that be okay?" she asked.

"Would what be okay?"

"To thank both of you at the same time."

Mikey's jaw went tight. His Adam's apple bobbed. He glanced in Rafe's direction, then closed his eyes and reopened them.

"Yeah," he said. "That'd be okay."

Rafe curled up behind her, his hips rocking against her ass. "Lube's in my bag."

Of course he'd brought that with him. Rafe was the sexual version of a Boy Scout, always prepared. Krissy crawled down the bed and leaned over the end of it, unzipping her roommate's duffle and searching around until she found the small bottle stashed inside.

Returning to her spot between them, she threw a glance at Rafe. He smiled placidly and waited, letting her take the lead.

Her pigtails falling over her shoulders, she leaned down to kiss Mikey, then lowered a hand and peeled off his briefs. His breathing went ragged as the fabric moved away and his cock pushed up to meet her touch. She'd felt the shape of him yesterday, but it was a new kind of thrill to get to see. He was long. Longer than Rafe, actually. And so hard Krissy needed to bite her lip, wondering how amazing he'd feel inside her.

Not yet. Maybe soon, but not yet.

On the other side of her, Rafe pulled off his boxers. Trying to figure out the mechanics, she nudged Mikey's thigh. "Sit up?"

He obeyed quickly, swinging his legs over the side of the bed. Rafe moved to flank her right, as if this were a pre-blocked scene and they already knew their marks.

And Mikey was staring at Rafe's cock.

It was hard not to look at, so thick and beautiful, and Mikey's chest rose and fell as his brows drew tight. There seemed to be some kind of battle raging inside him, something more he couldn't bring himself to say, but he wasn't stopping her. Just staring.

Her heart seized for a moment, but then Rafe put a hand on her arm and kissed her shoulder, a gentle encouragement. It ramped up her sex drive, tiny shivers unfurling along her skin. Popping open the bottle of lube, she drizzled the thick liquid over

Mikey's shaft until it coated him entirely, then turned and did the same to Rafe. It dripped along the ridge, chocolate sauce on the ice cream sundae of debauchery she'd created.

She placed the bottle behind her and reached for Rafe first. The wide circle she made with her fist around his girth was familiar territory, as was the low *Mmmm* he made at her first slow pump. Turning to Mikey, she leaned in for a kiss, then ran a finger around his tip.

He hissed, breaking the kiss as his head fell back. She did it again, finishing it off with a stroke downward, and his hips shot up into her touch. Anchoring himself with his hands behind him, Mikey moved in close, his forehead an inch away from hers, his shivery breaths warm on her face as she started a rhythm.

"Harder, Krissy," Rafe murmured. "I think we both need it harder."

"Jesus," Mikey breathed with another punch of his hips. "Yes. Harder. Please."

She did as Rafe instructed, and Mikey's eyes squeezed shut, face contorting into a mask of pleasured agony. Krissy worked them at an equal pace, high off the feeling of both of them in her fists, the sound of wet flesh against flesh. Her unhurried tempo earned her a nip at the shoulder from Rafe. He liked it faster, but she was holding him off, building him up, wanting to hear the crescendo of their pleasure at the same time.

It wasn't long before Mikey shuddered and went stiff. "Oh shit. *Shit*, I'm gonna come."

Rafe's warm chuckle was like the buzz of a vibrator, revving her up all over again. She felt his hand cover hers, taking control and jerking himself at the tempo he liked. Mikey opened his eyes, breath going hot and fast as he watched their fingers race over Rafe's cock. He swelled even harder under her ministrations, and that low noise in the back of his throat made an encore appearance, just like yesterday.

It was suddenly obvious to Krissy what Mikey wanted. And she could give it to him.

Her mouth at his ear, she whispered, "It's okay to want both of us, Mikey."

He exploded.

His eyes slammed shut, and he let out a groan. Krissy cupped her palm over his tip on every quick upstroke, gathering the sticky liquid that spurted into her hand as she helped him through it. One last grunt and he slumped against her. Rafe bit down on her other shoulder, and Krissy turned to watch as his release hit home. Warmth spilled over their hands, and Rafe moaned against her skin, then soothed the sting of his bite with a kiss.

Krissy tilted her head back and closed her eyes, almost laughing from the sheer joy bubbling up inside her, and the deep, hot craving for more. Making them come like that, having them at her mercy—it was like nothing she'd ever experienced.

She could go all over again.

Letting Mikey's softening shaft go, she draped her hand along his inner thigh, but his eyes were still shut, his sweaty forehead pressed to her arm. The mattress to her right rose as Rafe stood.

"*Towel*," he mouthed, and strode out of the room. Mikey clung to her, still catching his breath, too wrung out from his orgasm to move, she guessed.

Rafe returned a moment later with a towel wrapped casually around his waist. He tossed Krissy another one. "I don't know about you two, but that tuckered me out. I'm gonna shower and pass out. I'll take the couch tonight."

He winked and left the room. Krissy glanced after him, wistful. A small part of her thought it might've been nice to have all three of them sleep together, but that wasn't what he'd been after, and it would be good to have some time alone with Mikey after what had just happened.

She pressed her lips to the top of his head. "You okay?"

He shrugged. Pulled away from her and put his face in his hands.

Oh, no.

"Is something wrong?" she asked.

Mikey shook his head. "No. I don't know. Can we just...go to sleep?"

Worry popped the balloon she'd been floating on. "Sure," she croaked.

Not knowing what else to do, Krissy wiped her hands off, then offered the towel to Mikey. He took it from her and cleaned himself up, staying silent as he tossed it in a laundry basket, then reached for his briefs. She moved with him in silence, putting her underwear on too. Mikey lifted the blanket, and she crawled in beside him, curling her body around his when he shut off the light.

What had gotten him so upset? Yeah, a virgin having a three-way was definitely jumping in the deep end, but he'd seemed into it when they started. He'd been on board all the way through, until she said what she did at the end.

It's me. I made him do this. He's upset because of me.

She tried to talk herself out of it, but it wasn't working. Her anxieties were running away with her, her pulse in her throat, every limb tense. If she weren't wired already, the fact that he wouldn't talk to her was making it even worse. She had no idea how she was going to repair things, let alone sleep now.

She pressed a tentative hand to his chest, and he covered hers with his in the darkness. It was a small reassurance, but Krissy couldn't help but think what they'd done—this thing that she'd been dreaming about and had been so damn good—had just ruined everything.

SEVEN

It was a little after dawn when Mikey broke out of sleep again, body cold with night sweats, his chest so tight he could barely breathe. The guilt was too much. Even Krissy's warm body curled around his couldn't stop the panic wreaking havoc in his gut.

He gazed down at her sleeping form. She was so peaceful, all creamy skin and dark lashes. Being in here with her was what he'd been waiting for, her hands on him what he'd craved, but the memories of how much more he'd wanted last night were making his skin crawl.

He'd wanted Rafe too. And Krissy knew it.

Even worse? He'd taken the Lord's name in vain in the middle of it all, so turned on by his fucked-up desires it wrenched words he'd never normally say from him.

God, he was never going to be able to get these ideas out of his head, was he? He'd thought if he could make things work with Krissy, maybe he'd never have them again. But the part of him he'd hoped to bury with her arrival was far from gone. It was alive in every frazzled nerve ending. And despite the encouragement she'd given him in the heat of the moment, the euphoria of his orgasm had ended, and all Mikey could feel was shame.

He needed to get out of here.

He gingerly pulled the covers back and disentangled himself from Krissy's embrace. After searching for his glasses and finding them on the nightstand, he grappled with his clothes, losing his balance several times as he struggled to tug his pants on in the dim light of the room. Finally dressed, he stumbled into the bathroom, did his business, and tiptoed toward the front door. He'd just grabbed his coat when he heard Rafe's deep breathing.

He didn't want to look—was halfway pleading with himself not to—but he was a moth drawn to a flame, unable to stop himself. His coat in his hand, Mikey slowly turned around.

Rafe was naked from the waist up, the blanket bunched down low over his hips as he slept facedown on the futon. A tattoo covered the length of his back, a design Mikey had only gotten a glimpse at the night before. He took several unsteady steps toward the couch, curious and terrified as he bent closer to examine Rafe's ink.

A large heart spanned the space between his shoulder blades. The left side was red and white, embellished with magnificent feathers; the other black with webbed, scaly wings. A halo with two horns sat above it. The design ended at the base of his spine with the heart's dual sides twining together, black lines curling around into a forked tail.

Devil and angel, merged together. Was Rafe here to save him or to damn him?

Mikey threw on his jacket and hurried outside. Letting the door click shut behind him, he fumbled for his gloves, tugged on his hood, then raced down the steps and onto the street. It was so fucking backward, to be running away from where he usually went for solace, but now there was only one place he could think to go to for consolation.

His hands were like ice, his cheeks numb when he finally yanked open his church's front door. The heat after the six-block walk was welcoming, as were the empty pews he found inside. Monday morning mass had just ended and the next one wasn't until noon. The priest would be busy, and the odds of any of Mikey's students being here were slim to none, but he kept his head down anyway as he charged up the stairs to the second-floor balcony and sat in the back row.

His hood still up, he bent over, clasped his hands together, and stared out across the sanctuary to the crucifix.

I'm going to Hell.

Terror clutched Mikey's windpipe. He didn't want to think it, but the idea that God couldn't love anyone who didn't follow His teachings had been drilled into Mikey since he was old enough to read. It was what had kept him from approaching his crush in college, doing nothing but yearn from afar.

Knowing he'd never crossed that line had been his only saving grace—the one thing he could fall back on for consolation when he feared God's wrath. He'd come clean in confession and had been absolved from his transgressions, but now for the first time in his life Mikey was worried his luck had run out.

He drew in a shallow breath and pressed his knuckles to his forehead. Repentance was still an option. He hadn't actually done anything last night, other than feel and watch. He wasn't committing a sin if he didn't act on these desires.

But he *wanted* to.

There was no escaping it. It wasn't virgin curiosity driving his attraction to men, not a one-time feeling he'd had years ago that he'd get over when he found the right girl. He'd thought Krissy might be that girl—heck, he still did—but being with her hadn't changed anything.

Damn it, why couldn't he have been satisfied with her attention instead of craving them both?

His eyes closed, Mikey began singing silently, running through all the hymns he could think of about forgiveness, ones about penance and contrition and asking for mercy. He stayed that way for what must've been hours, trying to wash away his thoughts with song, not moving when people started filing in downstairs, hoping absolution would find him.

The only one who found him was Krissy.

He bolted upright when she sank onto the bench next to him, immediately cringing from the soreness in his back after so much time spent hunched over. She didn't say anything, her coat by her side. Mikey pulled off his hood and pushed his hair out of his eyes.

"How'd you know where I was?"

"I had a hunch." Her eyes were downcast, her face pale. Dressed in jeans and a simple blue sweater, she was the most subdued he'd ever seen her.

Mikey swallowed and glanced behind her. "Is Rafe with you?"

"He wouldn't be comfortable here."

The comment irked him. Given Rafe's apparent ease with his own bisexuality and casual feelings toward sex, Mikey supposed her roommate had plenty of reasons to feel on edge in a church, but Rafe's beliefs weren't his concern. What did concern him was Krissy, and the distance camped between them like a heavy morning fog.

There was no way they'd be able to fix this now.

She stayed quiet for a long time, then finally said, "I don't blame you for hating me."

"You think I hate you?" he asked. She nodded mutely. "Why?"

"Because it was my fantasy, what we did last night, and I pushed you into it when you weren't ready." She shook her head and pinched her eyes shut. "I'm sorry."

Mikey's stomach roiled. He didn't want to discuss this here, but she was hurting too, and he couldn't stand how sad she looked.

"I could never hate you."

Her eyes fluttered open. "You couldn't?"

"Of course not. And you didn't force me to do anything. This, me being here—" he sighed and waved around the room, "—that's my stuff, not yours."

One of her shoulders curled up in a shrug. "I think maybe we've both got some stuff we still haven't told each other."

"Maybe." Mikey drew in a deep breath as she slid closer to him on the bench.

"Was I right, last night?" she asked quietly. "About you wanting—"

"Yes." He couldn't let her finish that sentence. Not here. "You were."

"So, you're bi," she confirmed. Mikey could barely nod in reply. "Is that the real reason you're a virgin?"

"Partly, I guess. I'm not the type of guy the girls come running for, and I'm kinda shy, in case you haven't noticed." She giggled softly. The sound was a soothing balm to his ragged and flayed nerves. "But, yeah, it's that too. I haven't been able to come to terms with everything I..." he exhaled, "...want."

"When did you figure it out?"

He huffed out a laugh. Man, she asked a lot of questions. But it took the sting out of the situation, somehow. Like it wasn't anything serious, just more stuff she wanted to know.

"College. I dated a few girls and definitely liked them, but then my senior year, I met this guy. He was in my music history class and a little like you, actually. Really bubbly and full of life." She turned her smile into his shoulder. It gave him the strength to keep going. "We were paired up on a project, and the next thing I knew I was thinking about him all the time."

"Did anything happen?" The devilish glint in her eyes made his already queasy stomach sour.

Had he acted on his desires? Expressed the sudden consuming need to take another man's cock in his mouth? Partaken in the forbidden acts that drove him to quick, sweaty orgasms in his dorm room, imagining fucking into his crush from behind and losing his virginity in a totally different way?

"No."

"Why not?"

He looked at the bronze cross looming at the other end of the room. Life-sized and lit up where it hung beneath the domed ceiling, a white glow illuminated the figure suspended from it.

"It's an abomination."

His words came out in a whisper. Krissy's response, however, did not.

"What?" The word echoed in the empty room. Mikey winced.

"'You shall not lie with a male as one lies with a female,'" he said. "They're God's words. And I've never figured out how to interpret them differently."

"So you think this—" she lifted a missal from the rack and waved it around, "—two-thousand-year-old book that's been translated and edited and retranslated is actually the word of God?"

His cheeks went hot at her censure. The same disdain had driven him from the support group back at school.

He took the tome from her hands and put it back in its shelf. "That's not actually the Bible. It's a hymnal. But yeah."

She ducked her chin. "Sorry."

"No, it's—" He sighed. He didn't want her feeling bad. He wanted her to know him. To be understood by *somebody*, for once. "Were you ever teased as a kid?" At her nod, he said, "Me too. All the time. I didn't have a lot of friends. Fourth grade was awful—bullies on the bus, on the playground. I was so lonely. It got better after I met Dean."

"That was when you met?"

"I helped him with an answer to a question our teacher put him on the spot with, and that was it, friends for life. When Connor moved to town in high school and befriended me too, I felt invincible. But kids still bothered me when they weren't around." Mikey looked at the stained-glass windows, the ornate ceiling decorated with artwork. "Here, I got away from that. No one picked on me, and I never felt alone. I felt safe. Felt God's love. So yeah, I believe His word is in the Bible. I believe He's up there and is looking after us. It's a lot more lonely to believe there's no one in Heaven than to think there's a God who's simply asking me to follow His laws."

Krissy went silent for a moment, then asked, "So if you believe in God, and God created you, didn't he make you this person?"

Mikey sighed. It was a rationalization he'd used a hundred times before. He was born this way, God had decreed it, blah blah blah.

"What do you believe?"

She shrugged. "I believe there's a God. At least I think I do. Everything I was taught about religion was simply stories—the Bible and Mother Goose and Disney all mixed together, tall tales with a moral at the end. This is just a pretty room to me." She glanced at the ceiling. "I bet it has great acoustics though."

A short laugh burst out of Mikey's lungs. Her humor sent relief sputtering through him like heat coming off a rusty radiator. "That's actually what I like best about it here."

"The music?"

"Yeah. Getting a bunch of kids to sing something spiritual is practically a celestial event." But there was no way he could do that full time. Not when his thoughts were so unholy. "This place...it makes me feel like I belong. It's where I still feel a connection to God, even if what I want is so wrong."

"You think what we did last night was wrong?"

He couldn't answer that. Didn't want to. It wasn't fair to her. "I can't be bi, or gay, or—" he swallowed. Poly? Was that the term for what he was craving now? "—anything other than straight, and work here."

"Couldn't you work at another church? One that's a little more forward-thinking?"

Mikey responded with a sharp shake of his head. There were a few parishes in town that boasted their acceptance, rainbow pride flags hanging on the doors, but there was no anonymity when you were a Pelletier in Portland.

"People would talk. Word would get out. The company would suffer."

Her brow creased. "I don't understand."

"My parents don't want me to be openly bisexual because they think it'll make them lose customers."

Her mouth fell open. "That's crazy."

"It's not. Sure, there's a local LGBTQ community, but there's the opposite side too. Parishioners here who talked about the marriage equality act like it was the beginning of the apocalypse. If I chose to be with a guy, *it could hurt the business.*" He whispered the last bit, imitating his mother, then sighed. "We've been arguing over it since I came out to them. Well more like they lecture, I listen until I can't take it anymore. That's why I'm always at Dean's."

It was the other reason why his money sat in the bank. In case it ever got to be too much at home and he needed to bail.

Krissy shook her head. "You have a lot more in common with Rafe than you realize."

Something unlatched inside Mikey. A door he was afraid of

opening, a strain easing, but he wasn't ready for it. It didn't matter, though, because she was on to her next question.

"Do Dean and Connor know?"

Mikey often wondered if his buddies had a hunch about his orientation, but they'd never asked.

"I don't think so. And my parents aren't trying to be awful. It's not *just* about the business. They don't want my life to be difficult. They're trying to look out for me. And they paid for my college tuition and keep a roof over my head, so if I can make their lives easier, I want to."

If there was one commandment he believed in, it was the one about how to treat your parents. Honor thy father and mother and all.

Krissy sighed and leaned back on the bench. "Well, you're not the only one trying to please your parents."

"What do you mean?"

She wrinkled her nose. "I don't actually like yoga. I do it because my family asked me to, mostly since my therapist said it would help, but spending an hour in goddess pose doesn't exactly cure an anxiety attack."

He laughed, but it wasn't funny.

"I want to prove to them I'm okay, so I'm following the plan we all agreed to, even though my parents' daily phone calls make me bonkers. Every day I have to rate my symptoms on a one-to-ten scale: 'No, I haven't had any mood spikes today. Yes, I remembered my pills.' Whenever my sister comes to visit, she checks me over like I'm some specimen in a lab, and the way they all say 'maybe acting isn't the best idea' does wonders for my confidence." Krissy rolled her eyes, then shook her head. "I think they're afraid of me— of what could happen if I have another episode. It's because they care, but it's not so awesome when the people who are supposed to love you make you feel like a patient fresh from the psych ward."

She made a face on the words *psych ward*, big violet eyes going wide, and the heavy reminder of what she'd been through pelted Mikey like hail. She'd undergone so much, yet she could still be silly, her smile pressing at her cheeks.

She was so damn beautiful.

"I started picking up the pieces the summer I met Rafe," she continued. "He was the first person who made me feel like I was more than a walking, talking illness."

Mikey had yet to hear the finer points of how they'd gone from friends to lovers. He wasn't sure he wanted to. "But Rafe prefers men."

"It's just the way his cookie crumbles."

A cute joke, but now it was his turn to ask questions. "So why are you in this with him? Not that he's not...attractive, but why aren't you with someone who can be with you for real?"

The smile fell away from her face.

"I haven't been stable enough for a relationship. I feel things too hard, like when I met you. I wanted to be with you *so* much, so quickly. My emotions can overwhelm me, and my anxiety can be pretty intense. I've usually got this nonstop buzz of worry going on in my head, like an AM radio stuck on a news station. If I avoid relationships, I have a better chance at avoiding the cycles."

"Cycles?"

"The highs and lows. When I get happy, I'm super happy. When I'm down, I get incredibly depressed. Black holes, my therapist calls them. Like I'm at the bottom of a dark pit and I can't climb out. I try to steer clear of that, but even still, sometimes I don't know when I'm having a bad day like anyone else or when I'm manic. I'm always asking myself, is this the bipolar talking or is it me? And then there's the sex part."

She chewed on her pink, plump lower lip. He was *not* going to get a hard-on in church. He *wasn't.*

"What sex part?"

She wound her hands together. "The week I was hospitalized, I slept with a lot of guys. Five, I think. The doctors said it was because I was hypersexual—a symptom of the disease. I didn't believe it at first because I was always pretty sexually curious, but looking back, they were right." She sighed. Her leg bounced ceaselessly. "I brought one of the guys back to my dorm room and had sex with him right in front of my roommate. I called her to try and apologize, but she never called back. She won't even talk to me now."

"But it's not your fault. You know that, right?"

The half shrug she gave him proved she didn't.

"It's not like you had any control over it," he said. "It's something in your brain. There's nothing you need to ask forgiveness for."

Krissy cocked her head to the side and pointed to the crucifix. "That's true for you too."

Mikey reached out and lowered her hand. He appreciated the sentiment, but his issues were...different.

"Anyway," she continued. "Pleasure-seeking behavior is an indicator of an upswing, so I keep my sex drive locked up inside me, like a wild animal in a cage. Rafe crawls into it and lets me play in a way that's safe. I mean, the fact that we don't actually fuck could be why I'm even more wound up, but it helps."

Mikey could sense her restless energy, her all-too-familiar shame over desires. He'd thought that was his cross to bear, but knowing she carried something similar loosened some of the tension between his shoulders.

"I understand why you didn't tell me about it. Him." Mikey shook his head. "You."

She offered him a meek smile, and he held his hand out. Krissy curled hers around it, then leaned her head on his arm.

"Do your parents know?" he asked. "About you and Rafe?"

"Ohhh, no. They think he's gay."

"And they're okay with that?"

Her upward glance had her tiny, sharp chin digging into his biceps, but he didn't mind.

"Yes," she replied, her tone gentle. "It's why they let me move in with him. If anything, they see Rafe as safer. They'd see him as one giant symptom if they knew what was really going on." She leaned her head back against his arm. "I've told them a version of the truth: that I'm not ready for a relationship, and I prefer spending my time with him."

It was a lot to absorb as it was, but the last line snagged at him, a weed he couldn't pull.

"If you don't want a relationship, what do you feel about me?" he asked. "What did last night mean?"

She sat up and turned sideways on the bench but kept their hands together, her eyes on his palm. "When I was a kid, my parents sent me to circus camp. The thing that scared me the most was the trapeze."

She walked her fingers along his as she talked. A touch over every indentation, like she needed to focus on something other than her words.

"I loved swinging, but I was scared to let go, afraid the instructor on the other bar wouldn't catch me. He kept telling me to turn my brain off, let myself fly, but I couldn't. When I finally listened to him and flew off the bar, it was incredible. That place between trapezes, when you're soaring and not holding onto anything—it was the most free I'd ever felt, and I realized how silly it was to have been scared, because there was always someone there to catch me."

She stopped moving her hand and looked up. Hey eyes were filled with so much raw emotion, it cut straight through him.

"Being with you and Rafe last night, it was like that again. Like flying. Most of the time I'm chained to this disease, keeping myself rigid and sticking to my routine, but with the two of you there to catch me, I let go and felt...free."

It wasn't exactly an answer, but *wow*. He couldn't believe he'd made her feel like that.

Mikey smiled, leaned in, and whispered, "I hate the circus."

Krissy laughed—guffawed was more the word to describe it—and Mikey beamed at having brought some humor into the situation, at the brightness that had returned to her face. She squeezed his hand.

"Thank you for not hating me."

"Never was an option." If anything, he was starting to realize he felt completely the opposite.

Her hand still laced with his, she grabbed her jacket and stood, swinging her arm so his moved too. "Any chance you're ready to go back to the apartment?"

Something pressed at Mikey, an envious clench in his stomach over Krissy and Rafe's situation that didn't quite fit anymore. If anything, he wanted to be...part of it?

"What do Rafe and I have in common?"

She shook her head. "It's not my story to tell. You'll have to ask him."

Behind her, sunlight cascaded through the windows, lighting up her hair and shoulders, making her glow like his own personal guardian angel. Mikey wasn't prepared to face Rafe, but anything he was looking for at this point couldn't be found in a church. And he wasn't sure it was absolution he wanted anymore.

He stood up next to her. "Yeah. Let's get out of here."

EIGHT

Rafe was relaxing on the armchair when Mikey and Krissy entered the apartment. He looked up from his phone, the outline of his muscular form visible beneath his dark jeans and long-sleeved white tee. He'd trimmed his beard and mustache while they were gone, and the clean lines by his sideburns made the angles of Rafe's face even sharper, so masculine Mikey could feel it in his bones.

"Everyone cleansed of their sins now?"

His voice was sex and hot chocolate and a blanket on a cold day.

"I'm better now," Mikey said. "Thank you."

"Good. Although I personally found the idea of confession so ridiculous," Rafe said as he stood. "It's like the religious version of the Staples Easy Button. Bang! You're forgiven."

Mikey chuckled. It was difficult not to laugh at the other man's sarcasm. But Rafe's gaze remained trained on him, and Mikey had to pause for a moment, his heartbeat skittering at the barely masked concern couched in those dark eyes. It caught him by surprise, but Mikey shook it off, taking Rafe's look in the spirit he was sure it had been meant. He should've realized Rafe would be bothered by his disappearance too, given the state it put Krissy in.

"Sorry I bolted. I didn't mean to worry you both."

Rafe grinned. "It's cool. I was only pissed because you have the truck keys, and we've got a theater tour to get to."

Krissy released Mikey's hand and clapped. "I almost forgot. Let's go!"

As she skipped to the door, Rafe and Mikey exchanged glances. Rafe dipped his chin, a small move that said *we cool now?* Mikey nodded. It was an odd moment, one that was comforting and reminded him there was some kind of common ground between them.

As well as the fact that they'd seen each other naked.

They went down to the truck and made their way into the Old Port. The sidewalks were coated with chunks of snow and dirt, the already-darkening sky dappled with clouds. The doors to the theater were unlocked, and Mikey followed Krissy and Rafe inside.

"How'd Merrick work this out?" he asked. "Aren't they getting ready for tonight's show?"

"It's Monday," Krissy answered. "The theater's dark today."

"You've arrived!"

They all looked up the stairs. Merrick was at the landing by the mezzanine seats, sans the long black wig he'd worn in the performance. His natural hair was spiked and red, his ears a veritable Christmas tree of piercings. He slid down the banister and landed in front of Krissy, holding out his hand.

"Are you ready for your tour, madame?"

She giggled. "I am, fair sir."

He hooked her arm around his. "Good. The cast is waiting for you."

"They didn't take the day off?"

"Of course not. We're theater people. We are each other's family. The stage is our home." Merrick glanced over his shoulder at Rafe. "Right, Rafael Elias Brigham?"

That was Rafe's full name? It was quite a mouthful. Faith-inspired too.

Rafe chuckled. "Right, Godfrey Merrick the Third."

Merrick winced and mimed a gag. "Don't call me that."

He turned with a flourish and led Krissy toward the stage. Mikey hung a few paces back as he and Rafe followed them down the aisle, wanting to give Krissy room to explore.

And daring to explore a little himself.

"How do you and Merrick know one another?"

Rafe took off his coat and draped it over his arm. "We were lovers," he replied simply. "It didn't work out, but we parted on good terms." His brow was creased, his smile a bit further away than usual. "He was the first person I met when I got to New York. Made me feel like I had a home there."

"You didn't have one anymore in Georgia?"

Mikey knew he was being nosy, but he figured seeing the guy's junk meant it was okay to ask about his hometown.

Rafe's pace slowed. He worked his jaw, as if he were recalling a punch and was testing to see if the spot was still tender. "No. My parents gave me my full inheritance as long as I promised to go away and never come back."

Mikey's heart stuttered, as did his footsteps. "What?"

Rafe stopped too, his eyes diamond hard. "They banished me because I wasn't able to pray the bi away."

Oh. Shit. "What did they do to you?"

Rafe dipped his head and continued walking.

"I was raised Baptist, in the kind of church where being gay is considered a disease, or demonic possession. When I realized I liked men too, I pleaded for God to take it away from me. I thought if I prayed harder, the change would happen. It didn't, of course, and the summer before I started at NYU, I asked my parents for help. They told me my feelings were 'sinful but curable'." Rafe launched into a brash southern accent as they ascended the few quick steps onto the stage. "'Give your heart to the Lord, and walk *away* from temptation.'"

Gone was the jovial, confident persona Mikey had assumed was the other man's natural state. The timbre of Rafe's voice chilled him to the bone.

"They signed me up for three weeks of what they called therapy." Rafe leaned against the wall and tightened his grip on his coat. "I made it through one before popping out my razor in the bathroom."

Mikey swallowed. He'd heard about reparative therapy, about the things done to people in places like that. He glanced at Rafe's wrists and whispered, "You tried to kill yourself?"

"Tried. And failed. At least that's what my parents told me when they came to the hospital. They said I was cowardly and selfish. That I'd failed them. Failed God. They didn't care how I felt. They just wanted me gone."

Rage ignited in Mikey's chest—a helpless futility that he couldn't protect Rafe from what he'd been through. Fix it, somehow. But Rafe didn't look like he needed fixing. He lifted his chin in a move of defiance Mikey had never been brave enough to make.

"They released me, the disgraced prodigal son. I left home, went to New York, and never looked back. Now I embrace who I am and don't question it, for anyone."

Mikey shook his head, respecting the hell out of the guy. It was unimaginable, enduring what Rafe had, and still being able to stand here and tell the tale.

"I'm so sorry. My parents have been pretty lousy, but it's been nothing like that."

Rafe's lips quirked up into a smirk. "I was wondering when you were going to tell me."

Time seemed to slow as Mikey's breathing sped up, his heart pounding. He wondered if he needed to clarify that he was bi, not gay, but he had a feeling Rafe already knew. Their eyes locked, and if they'd been alone, Mikey might have let Rafe kiss him.

He might've been the one to do it first.

"I guess I just did."

Rafe's brows lifted, his eyes dancing, but then Krissy scampered toward them with a radiant, breathless smile.

"Merrick wants to get me in makeup and a costume."

"What, you're not wearing one already?" Rafe asked. Krissy blew a raspberry at him, and he tousled her hair. "I'm kidding. Go on. Dress up for us."

She glanced at Mikey. Waiting for his consent too, it seemed. "Do it. I can't wait to see."

Krissy beamed and dashed toward the curtain, ducking behind it along with Merrick and a female cast member. Mikey and Rafe crossed to follow her.

"I'm glad Merrick was able to do this," Rafe said. "I was worried yesterday soured everything for her."

"Krissy can't be around smoke because of her condition?"

Mikey wasn't sure if he should broach the topic, but Krissy hadn't expressly said he couldn't, and it was too late to undo asking it anyway.

"It's more in her head than anything else. Smoke isn't going to trigger anything, but it makes her uneasy. Reminds her of her first episode. I shelter her from stuff as much as I can, but honestly? Sometimes it sucks. I haven't taken a puff in years."

"You smoke pot?"

"Used to with Merrick back in the day." The coy look on Rafe's face was suggestive and alarming. "You?"

"Never." Mikey had never smoked anything, not even a cigarette. "Always wondered what it would be like though."

He thought it might be close to Krissy's experience on the trapeze. Sometimes, when he'd escaped an argument with his parents, he wanted to clock out mentally, to disconnect from reality entirely. He'd thought about asking Dean or Connor how to get some drugs, figuring they'd know, but stopped himself. He wanted to be a good Christian, and that was one more unethical activity he kept himself from.

They stepped from the threshold of the stage and into the wings. A clipboard with cues scratched across it hung from the wall, hooks with body mikes next to it. Set pieces cluttered a hallway that ran perpendicular to the stage. Krissy was at the other end of it, her head thrown back as Merrick swept her into one of the dressing rooms. The sound of her laughter put a goofy grin on Mikey's face. Rafe's smile wasn't so different from his own.

"You two are close." It wasn't a statement that needed confirming, but Mikey wanted to hear it from him.

Rafe put his coat on the floor and sat next to it. Mikey sank down beside him.

"After we found out about our...shared experiences, it was like fate. Not everyone knows what it's like to be on meds for depression." He examined his wrist. "Or to be on the inside of a mental hospital."

Oh.

Rafe dropped his hand and let his head fall back against the wall. "She's like family to me. The only family I have now. We've got the same scars, just from different kinds of battles. That's why I hope she likes it here." He looked over at Mikey. "Why I hope she'll audition for this company."

The last sentiment was clear: *Why I hope she'll stay here with you.*

"You don't want her to live with you anymore?"

"I do. I'll miss her like crazy, but I want her with someone who can give her everything."

I.e., him. "Because you only fall for men?"

Rafe's eyes twinkled with merriment. "Are you taking Krissy's place here?"

Mikey blushed. Why *was* he asking so many questions? But he needed the answers.

"I guess. I mean, I just wanted to know if that's why you and Krissy don't..."

"Have actual sex?" When Mikey nodded, Rafe shrugged, his cheerful expression fading. "I suppose it's the last vestiges of a religion I've thrown off. It's ridiculous considering the circumstances, and the fact that I had plenty of partners before her, but to me, sex means commitment. It means I'm going to stick by you forever. It means love, and I can't give her that. But that's not the only reason I hold back from her."

A flurry of movement by the dressing rooms caught their attention. Doors opened and closed, Krissy's voice ringing out as Merrick tugged her down another hallway. Rafe turned his head, fixated on the ghost of Krissy's presence.

"She puts on a good show, but she's not as strong as she seems. She needs someone to be there for her. Even if I could give her all my heart, I'm not in great mental shape either. What happens to her if I go under?"

The soft cadence of his voice made Mikey feel like he was finally getting a glimpse of the real Rafe. And of how much he cared for Krissy's welfare.

Before either of them could say anything else, music blasted through the theater's speakers—a radio playing the haunting opening to Madonna's "Like a Prayer". Rafe went quiet and smiled.

"You like Madonna?" Mikey asked.

Rafe listened for another moment, then hopped to his feet and peeked around the curtain. "That's not Madonna."

He pulled the heavy black fabric back, and Mikey moved to stand. It wasn't the radio they were hearing. It was Krissy, alone in the spotlight in a frilly red dress, the pit band playing with her. Her voice was pure and clear, no trace of stage fright anywhere as she belted out the song.

"Holy shit," Mikey murmured. "She's amazing."

"Isn't she?"

Rafe flashed a grin back at Mikey before running out to the stage. He sang the second verse with her, spinning her around before pulling her back to his side. Their moves were effortlessly coordinated, with the kind of ease only people familiar with one another's bodies could have. The lyrics couldn't have been more perfect either. It certainly felt like a dream, being here with them, and as the rest of the cast joined in, Mikey stood by the curtain, transfixed. He was in awe of Krissy's and Rafe's talent, of their bravery, of the way they'd both risen up from the ashes of experiences that could've destroyed them.

Krissy turned back and reached a hand out, gesturing for Mikey to join them. He hesitated, then kicked his doubts to the curb. He wanted nothing to do with the guilt that had crippled him this morning. He wanted inside whatever this crazy situation with them was, to bask in their attention, in their openness and desires.

He walked onto the stage and put his arm around her. Fitting it snugly above Rafe's, he let the pleasure of touching them both roll through him.

Forgive me, Father, for I have sinned.

And I want to do it again.

* * *

THEY RETURNED to the apartment a few hours later. The cast had ordered in dinner after Krissy's performance, and they'd shared a meal as well as more impromptu songs. Mikey had joined in, taking a guitar offered by one of the musicians, and they'd left with an invitation from Merrick to join him at a karaoke bar on New Year's Eve.

They climbed the steps to the entrance. Mikey opened the door, but Rafe hovered on the landing.

"I think I'll hang out here a bit. Take in the view."

"The *view?*" Krissy asked. "It's pitch black out. And freezing." She stepped into his space and peered up at him. "Why are you being weird?"

"I'm not."

"You are."

It made him uneasy, watching them argue. Mikey would've felt like he was intruding, if it weren't for the way Rafe's gaze sneaked toward his.

"I thought I'd give the two of you some space. And—" he sighed and pulled a small baggie from his pocket, "—Merrick gave me a couple of real joints. I'm sorry. I didn't want to upset you and it's...been a while."

Krissy bowed her head. Mikey wanted to console her, then to yell at Rafe for putting her in this position, for bringing something into the apartment he knew would make Krissy uncomfortable, but this seemed like it was between them.

And a small, horrible part of him wanted to smoke with Rafe too.

"Forget it. I'll throw them out," Rafe said, but Krissy cut him off.

"No," she said sharply. "Smoke inside, just do it by the window or something." She looked back at Mikey. "Would Dean and Jamie mind?"

"Doubtful." If Dean had given Mikey permission to have sex

in his bed, he didn't think a little pot in the living room would matter.

"Then it's settled. I'll do my yoga in the bedroom."

Rafe blinked at her, his brow furrowed. "You sure?"

"Yeah. It's your vacation too." She brushed past Mikey and curled her fingers around his arm. "Can I talk to you for a sec?"

"Sure." Leaving Rafe behind them, he let her tow him down the hall and into the bedroom. "What's—"

She was kissing him before he'd finished talking. Hard, aggressive kisses, her tongue sliding along his as she pushed him against the wall and dug her fingers into his hair. She rocked her lower body against his, and Mikey moaned into her mouth, too surprised to think clearly enough to ask if she was okay and too turned on to care.

He skated his touch over the curve of her waist, thumbs inching under her clothes to sweep along her sides. Her skin was still cool from being outside. She kissed his neck, teeth skidding upward until she reached his ear.

"You can smoke too," she whispered. "I won't be mad."

"No, I...*shit*—" She bit down on his earlobe. "I thought I'd stay here with you."

"And watch me stretch? That sounds pretty boring." She inched her hands down his back. "Don't you want to go out there and relax?"

She gripped his ass, thumbs riding along the crack. His knees buckled. Fuck.

"I guess."

"Okay then." She let go of him and took a step back. "Have fun. I'll see you in a bit."

He pulled the door open, then paused. "You're really cool with this?"

"Yeah." She gave him a salacious smile. "I kinda like the idea of you all giggly and stoned."

Once she'd shut the door, Mikey leaned back against it, inhaling slowly. He'd expected her to need reassuring, not a make-out session before ushering him out of the room to do something that was illegal in half the country.

Hoping she was really as fine with everything as she seemed, Mikey headed into the living room. Rafe was standing at the window farthest from the bedroom. It was wide open, letting cold air in, the oven vent on full blast. One look over his shoulder had Rafe shaking his head.

"I'm guessing it wasn't talking Krissy wanted to do with you."

Mikey reached a hand up. His hair was a disheveled mess. "Do I look that bad?"

"Here." Rafe held out the joint he had pinched between this thumb and forefinger. "I think you need a hit more than I do."

Mikey took a step forward, huffing out a breath in embarrassment. His stomach pitched with excitement as he took what Rafe offered. It felt wicked and decadent, getting to share such an intimate thing with him. Something sexual but not quite, breathing the same air, their mouths on the same little piece of paper.

"I'm going to cough my head off once I take my first puff, aren't I?" he asked.

"Probably."

Mikey held the joint between his lips. One long, burning inhalation later, and he was hacking up his guts. Rafe's amused expression was barely visible from his watery eyes.

"I'm glad to see what an excellent influence our visit is having on you," Rafe said. "Welcome to the dark side."

It certainly felt like Mikey had crossed a line somewhere. Stepped over an invisible boundary he'd stayed away from. Once he was finally upright, he took another experimental puff, breathing in deeply. This time Mikey managed to keep most of the smoke in his lungs, exhaling without as much coughing. One more hit, and his body grew tingly, his head swimming with a lightheadedness he should've expected but somehow didn't. Mikey handed the joint back to Rafe.

He took a long drag and stared out the window. "One thing I forgot to mention earlier."

"What's that?"

"If you break Krissy's heart, I'll kill you."

Mikey snorted, then started giggling. Rafe cackled too, and it was a minute before they had control over themselves.

"I'm not exactly the heartbreaking type," he finally said.

"No?"

Mikey pointed at his chest. "Virgin, remember?"

"Right." Rafe blew smoke out the corner of his mouth. "Sorry I dragged that into the spotlight last night. I just never would've expected it."

Mikey felt himself flush at the compliment, warmth gathering in his chest. "I always worried it was plastered on my forehead."

"Not at all." Rafe's gaze flickered away, then back again. "Have you ever been with a guy?"

Tension sparked, delicious and dangerous. "Never."

"Is that why you ran out on us this morning?"

"That and my..." Mikey searched for words that wouldn't break the mood. There was an opportunity blooming here, something he was both terrified of and desperate not to miss out on. "Religious issues."

Rafe nodded, a move that showed a shared understanding. "But you're okay with what happened last night?"

Mikey tried to read the subtext, to figure out where Rafe was coming from, but he couldn't. The guy was an emotional fortress. "Are you?"

A flash of Rafe's impish smile returned. "Definitely."

Guh.

"I wasn't," Mikey said. "But I think I am now."

Rafe's gaze softened for a second—a brief, unguarded look Mikey didn't have the brainpower to work out—before he handed what was left of the blunt back to him. Their fingers brushed, and Rafe's touch was a high-voltage shock that found its way into Mikey's pelvis and tugged.

He took a final hit. Rafe plucked the joint from his hand and flicked it out the window.

"So." His voice was layered with a hint of something that made Mikey's skin go hot. "Krissy admitted her fantasy last night. What's yours?"

Guilt hovered but Mikey ignored it. In that moment, he didn't care about God or religion or his parents' opinions. He wanted the gentle play of Krissy's feminine curves alongside Rafe's masculine touch. Hard and soft together, hands and legs everywhere, mouths too, grinding, hot and wet.

An ecstatic, filthy revelry of sin.

"Something close to last night, actually. But with...more."

"More, huh?" Rafe smirked, and Mikey wasn't sure if it was the dirty look in the other man's eyes or the marijuana that was making his head spin.

"Yeah. A lot more."

A quiet groan caught their attention. Krissy was in the hallway, and the look on her face suggested she'd caught the last few lines of their conversation.

"You're all done with your yoga?" Rafe asked.

"I did enough."

He gave them both a leering grin, a sex god looking over his disciples.

"Watching you onstage inspired me today, Krissy," he said. "I think it's time I had my directorial debut. It's a scene I just came up with. I call it 'Deflowering Mikey'."

A thrill shivered through Mikey—half of him excited, the other half apprehensive as hell over the idea of who would be deflowering him. Before he could ask, Rafe strode toward Krissy, took her hand, and twirled her around with the same effortlessness he'd shown onstage. He trapped her against him, her back to his front.

"And you're going to be our prop."

She went still, her eyes seeming even wider from the stage makeup. "Is that what Mikey wants?"

"I don't know." Rafe slid his hands down to her hips, but his gaze landed on Mikey. "Is that what Mikey wants?"

Nerves hovered in the distance, his old fears lingering like the snow-thick clouds on the coast. But Mikey was tired of being restrained by the ideals he'd lived by. There was no denying how much he wanted this. He was practically shaking already, with the promise of pleasure in their words.

"Yes," he said.

Krissy blew out an uneven breath. "But are you sure this is how you want your..."

She ducked her chin, her doubts clear in the rough slant of her brow. Wanting to soothe her, Mikey stepped over to them and ran his knuckles over Krissy's cheek until her gaze lifted.

"Am I sure this is how I want my first time to be?"

She nodded, sadness and worry clouding her eyes. But she didn't need to worry that she was the one pushing him right now.

Dipping his head to breathe against her ear, he whispered, "I couldn't think of anything hotter."

A hard shudder shook every inch of her. Mikey kissed her, tongue skating past her lips and licking hers. He pulled back, and they shared a smile before he looked at Rafe. The other man's eyes glittered.

"I think the bedroom will do nicely for this scene," Rafe mused, then raked his teeth down Krissy's neck. Her hips kicked, a tiny reflex. "Go on, little prop. Into the bedroom with you."

Krissy's face lit up. Exuberant, she pulled away from him and scampered down the hall. Rafe gallantly swept an arm out, and Mikey held his gaze for a moment before following behind her. She'd yanked her clothes off by the time they reached the door. Rafe meandered in behind Mikey with one eye squinted, his hands in a square formation as he mimed searching for the perfect camera angle.

"This light will do nicely. Krissy, your first mark is on your back on the bed."

Eyes blazing, she did as she was told, her body parallel to the pillows. She spread her thighs open, knees up, feet flat on the bed. She raised her arms above her head in a move that lifted her small breasts, her cheeks ruddy with want.

Holy shit, this was happening. This was actually happening.

"Condoms, Mikey?" Rafe asked.

Mikey's hands shook when he opened the dresser drawer Dean had emptied for him and retrieved the plastic box he'd tucked away before Krissy's arrival, hoping for this.

Well, not exactly this. This was about a thousand times better.

Mikey deposited his glasses on the nightstand before turning back around. Rafe plucked the foil package from his hand.

"The scene begins with the young virgin looking over the girl offering herself to him. He knows he'll barely have to warm her up at all, with the way she's practically begging for it."

Rafe knelt next to Krissy and dipped his fingers between her splayed legs. She made a soft sound of pleasure, and Mikey needed to press a palm to his fly. He'd gotten painfully hard watching Rafe touch her the night before. He hadn't known he was a voyeur, but seeing this was almost hotter than the prospect of doing it himself.

Almost.

He pulled off his shirt, hands getting caught in the sleeves in his eagerness to be with them, then shucked his jeans and boxer briefs. Any uneasiness he'd felt the day before at being naked around Rafe was absent, replaced instead with a wild, animalistic craving. To touch and be touched too.

Krissy's gaze met Mikey's, her body undulating as Rafe glanced back at him.

"Look how hard Mikey is," he said. "I bet he can't wait to feel you. To see how wet you are."

The low, taunting sound of Rafe's voice combined with the blush racing from Krissy's cheeks to her breasts had Mikey's hands tingling. Rafe stepped aside, and Mikey moved in beside Krissy. He stroked her thighs, fingers light over her skin, then paused at her entrance, waiting. He wanted her permission, even if Rafe was running the show.

She nodded wildly. Mikey pushed two fingers in to the knuckle, pumping deep.

Krissy let out a mewl, a line forming between her eyebrows as her hips arched. Her stomach muscles bunched as he explored her, sliding in and out. She was slick and tight, burning up with heat, and he could only imagine how it would feel to be inside her. To finally, *finally* do this, and watch her reactions as he fulfilled her needs too.

He'd wrapped his other hand around his dick before he'd even realized it.

"I didn't say you could do that."

Rafe's chastisement drew Mikey's gaze upward. "You want to do it for me?" he asked with a strike of boldness he hadn't known he had in him.

Rafe gave Mikey a smug look, one side of his mouth curling up as he stroked a knuckle along Krissy's nipple. One tweak from him had her sucking back a breath, body clenching around Mikey's fingers.

"Up on your hands and knees, sweetheart. I want to see Mikey take you from behind."

Mikey shuddered and met Krissy's lust-soaked gaze as he slid his fingers free. She moved into position, and Mikey stood, taking a second to glance back at Rafe. He was still fully clothed, his erection apparent beneath his jeans.

"What about you?" Mikey asked. He wasn't sure what he was ready for, but he wanted Rafe's pleasure too.

Pocketing the condom, Rafe moved in behind him. Pressed his chest to Mikey's bare shoulder blades.

"What about me?" he asked, his voice like honey. "I'm the director here, and directors like to watch. I'll get mine from the two of you after. Besides, we both know how badly Krissy needs to get fucked."

She moaned, head falling between braced arms. One of Rafe's hands slid over his hip, and Mikey's mouth dropped open in a gasp. The three inches of height the other man had on him gave Rafe the perfect advantage, his lips at Mikey's ear.

"But if you want to know," he whispered, "I've been thinking about your mouth on me since I first saw you at the train station."

"Oh God." Mikey tilted his head back until he was looking at Rafe, and then their mouths crashed together, all hot lips and rough stubble and *Jesus fucking Christ.*

The words made guilt burn in his chest, but then all that vanished, his knees going rubbery and his mind going blank as Rafe palmed his other hip and squeezed.

His kiss was confident, stronger and more passionate than Krissy's. Mikey was too eager, too sloppy, but Rafe slowed him down, tongue chasing Mikey's back into his mouth with tiny teasing dips. He felt Rafe's hands moving over his pelvis, and Mikey's breathing went wild, his heart hammering against his ribs. He almost couldn't stand Rafe's slow taunt, fingers creeping inward one maddening inch at a time, until he gripped the base of Mikey's cock with one hand and stroked over it with the other.

"Fuck," Mikey rasped, breaking their kiss. "Oh, *fuck* yes."

He swayed backward, his weight on Rafe as everything got hot and blurry. The languid tugs of the other man's fist sent sparks of pleasure down his spine. Mikey dragged his eyes open, needing to see what Rafe was doing, and the way Krissy had her head tilted over her shoulder to watch too made everything worse. Or better—he wasn't sure. There was a fiendish glint in her eyes that grew wilder the same second Rafe stopped, hands moving to rip the condom open.

"Now you're both my props." Rafe rolled it slowly over Mikey's stiff flesh. His breath rushed out as Rafe began stroking him again, fingers making a perfect ring of tension over the latex barrier. "And I want to see both of you explode."

His hand still moving, Rafe prodded Mikey toward Krissy until the tip of his dick eased into her pussy. Barely half an inch of him was enveloped, and his eyes snapped shut, jaw tight as he groaned and fought to hold on. It was too much. The sensation of hot and tight, of Rafe's short, quick strokes as he jerked Mikey off. Jerked him off *into* Krissy. She whimpered, the tease of him barely inside obviously not enough, but Mikey was too far gone to help her.

"Not gonna last like this," he managed through gritted teeth.

Rafe nipped his earlobe. "That's the idea."

He urged Mikey another inch inside her, and Mikey nearly collapsed, hands dropping to grip Krissy's hips. A useless moan of protest rumbled from him when Rafe stopped stroking. He reached past Mikey, wrapped his hands around Krissy's thighs and pulled, drawing her slowly backward until she sheathed him entirely.

Mikey trembled—the wet clasp of her pussy was better than anything he'd ever imagined. As was the feeling of Rafe's erection, insistent against his ass. When he was fully seated, Krissy's head dropped on a quiet *yes*. She dug her hands into the blanket, and the picture of her pleasure was as hot as the snug warmth surrounding him.

Rafe started a slow rhythm, deliberately driving Krissy forward before pushing Mikey's hips to meet hers again. Sensation raced from Mikey's cock to his toes, his fingertips, his teeth. Trapped between their bodies, he watched Krissy move, fucking her at the pace Rafe set for them. When Rafe sped things up, Mikey knew he had seconds left. One more thrust, and he was lost.

His orgasm nearly ripped him in half. Mikey cried out, reaching blindly to grasp at them both. Rafe chuckled and bit down on his neck, a pinch of pain to balance out the insane pleasure. Mikey bent over, shoulders heaving with the force of his release. His head was still swimming when he pulled out, his vision clear enough to toss the condom in the trash and sink onto the bed. Krissy shifted around to face them, her hair a mess, eyes hooded and needy.

"Don't worry, sweetheart," Rafe said lowly. "I haven't forgotten you."

A shiver went through Mikey's exhausted body as Rafe stripped, tattoo leaping across his muscles, fearsome and beautiful. He crawled onto the bed and whispered something to Krissy. She nodded, her hunger and affection for him written all over her face. He kissed her tenderly, then more aggressively, one hand around her neck cleaving her to him, the other making teasing swirls over her hip.

Rafe ended the kiss with a nip to her lower lip. Lying down on his back, he manipulated her over him until his head was between her thighs. Her eyes drifted shut as Rafe's tongue drove into where Mikey's cock had just been. It was waking up already when she bent her head to take Rafe in her mouth.

Mikey watched them move, taking in every hitched breath, every pleasure-riddled grip of their hands, every roll of their hips.

They were gorgeous. Both of them.

Sitting up, Mikey dragged his fingertips over one of Rafe's thighs, the smattering of hair on his skin, then danced them along the curve of Krissy's back. Her body surged beneath his touch. Feeling a tiny bit of power course through him, he experimentally slid back until he grazed her wet flesh. Rafe shifted slightly, following Mikey's lead and giving him room. He could tell the exact second Rafe's lips closed over Krissy's clit by her muffled gasp.

That was a cue if he'd ever heard one. Mikey plunged his fingers inside her.

A whine came out around the sound of soft suction. The vibrations must've hit Rafe hard, because his hips lifted on a grunt. Fascinated, Mikey repeated the motion, and it caused another chain reaction—Krissy moaning, Rafe's body jolting in response. It was a potent thing, to control their pleasure like this, and Mikey kept up his tempo, working Krissy in tandem with Rafe until she shattered. Her head lifted with a sharp snap as she came, hard.

She slumped forward and rolled to the side with a satisfied smile. Licking her lips, she jutted her chin at Mikey, then nodded at Rafe.

Finish the job, her look said.

It was Mikey's last opportunity to back out, the final moment to reach for an escape hatch, mumble an apology, and back off.

He didn't want his demons haunting him anymore.

He lunged hungrily for Rafe, unsure of himself but driven by instinct as he gripped the other man's cock. Rafe was still slick from Krissy's mouth, and the feeling of the familiar shape in his palm, handling a dick that wasn't his own, was so taboo and hot that Mikey was rock hard all over again.

Rafe's hips rose into Mikey's fist, but he seemed more focused on Mikey's face than his hand—eyes soft, his mouth slightly agape as he gazed upward, the craftiness Mikey had so often seen in Rafe's expression replaced with something akin to...wonder?

He couldn't be sure, but a quick, shared glance between Rafe and Krissy had Rafe pushing Mikey's hand away and going up on his knees.

"Come here," he whispered roughly.

Mikey mirrored Rafe's position. One hand on the back of Mikey's neck, Rafe wrapped the other around both of them. The feeling of Rafe's cock against his, of flesh on flesh and Rafe's purposeful stroking, was driving him out of his mind. It was a damn good thing he'd come once already, because *fuck*. Mikey bowed his head to rest his forehead on Rafe's shoulder. Closing his eyes, he gave in, rocking into the other man's grip until Rafe's shudder and the hot spill of come propelled Mikey into a second orgasm, so intense his voice cracked when he moaned Rafe's name.

Sated, Mikey found his shirt to clean up with, then lay back against the pillows. Rafe followed suit, and a calm drowsiness pulled Mikey under until the sound of a soft moan had him dragging his eyes open. Krissy was smiling at him from her spot on the bed, one hand between her thighs.

"Is she touching herself?" Rafe asked, his eyes closed.

"Yup."

She bit her lip and smiled even wider, no shame at all in being caught.

"Krissy, you little brat!" Rafe shouted, but he was laughing. Mikey laughed too, until they were all clutching their stomachs in ecstatic, blissed-out hysterics.

She crawled in between them, that mischievous grin plastered on her face as her fingers dipped and swirled. It didn't matter if she needed to come again. She could need a thousand more orgasms, and it still wouldn't matter. He'd never felt so good, so happy and *right*, and Mikey wanted her pleasure.

Wanted Rafe's. Wanted to exist in a place where all that mattered was taking what he needed and giving it back to them. If this was the happiness that could be found in deviance, Mikey didn't know how he'd lived so long without it.

And God help him, he was going to enjoy the hell out of it now.

NINE

K rissy couldn't sleep, too wired hours after Mikey and Rafe had passed out on either side of her.

That was fine, though. She didn't need sleep. Sleep was for people who hadn't had the most incredible, sexually intense night of their lives. Who hadn't just rocked it on a stage full of strangers. She could've tried to go through her *shavasana* again since her meditation earlier had been a total bust, but she had no interest in attempting to quiet her mind right now. It was a risky mood to be in, but the feeling of swinging on that trapeze again was a high she wanted to ride on a little while longer.

She didn't want to risk waking Rafe and Mikey, though. Her boys needed rest if they were going to ravage her again in the morning.

Turning toward Mikey, she reached up and brushed a few strands of unruly hair off his forehead. He looked calm, so at ease, his sleeping countenance so different from the pain that had marred his features the day before in the church. Whatever amount Krissy's heart had ached when she'd learned about Rafe's past, it hurt twice as much now that she knew Mikey's. The fears he had about God and Hell, the burden his parents were putting on him—it wasn't fair. He was too sweet to carry that kind of weight. But here, now, he seemed free of all that.

She liked that she'd made that possible for him, even if she didn't know what came next.

Climbing silently out from between them, she groped around in the dark for her sweatshirt and panties, then found her cell and checked the time. A quarter to four, and she'd been staring at the ceiling since they turned out the light, cooking up more kinky scenarios for them to act out. She hadn't looked at her phone since they came back from the theater, and a bit of remorse stabbed when she saw her missed notifications.

You haven't logged your mood yet. How are you feeling right now?

Two of the same reminders read out on her screen, along with another, less benevolent notification: *Missed call from Mom and Dad.*

Shit. Not good.

She typed out a quick message to both their emails, scrounging up a lie about her phone going dead and it being too late to call them by the time she got a chance to charge it. She didn't like lying but it was the best she could do. At least she'd remembered to take her meds tonight.

No, wait, that was last night.

She cc'd her sister on the email before sending it out into cyberspace. After digging into her bag and finding her pills, she downed one with a swig of water from the bathroom sink and padded into the living room.

The piercing howl of wind dragged her attention to the windows. Outside, snow billowed toward the ground. A storm must've moved in during the last few hours. It was coming down heavily, sticking to the pavement in a way it rarely could on New York City's heated streets.

Krissy hauled up one of the windows, wanting to breathe in the cold, crisp air. Snowflakes painted her face, and when she braced her hands on the sill, her palm covered something small and square-shaped.

A matchbook, the words *Portland Repertory Theater* stamped on the side of it.

Krissy frowned. She'd been pissed at Rafe for bringing those joints from Merrick here, but being her sole support network had to be exhausting for him. If he kept up like this, hardly ever having any fun, he'd crack. It was like those masks on an airplane: you had to put one on yourself before helping others. Rafe needed to breathe.

So she'd sucked it up about the pot. She wasn't about to hold him back, or Mikey for that matter, which was why she'd insisted he smoke too. It was another thing she wanted to give him—a little break from how tightly wound he kept himself. She didn't feel bad about being left out, as long as she was a part of them enjoying themselves after.

And enjoy themselves they had. Twice—the second time with her riding Mikey while Rafe knelt behind her, one hand on her clit as the other did things to Mikey she couldn't see but made him curse and squirm and beg for more.

Pure sexual deviance. She would've felt guilty if it had been any other guys, but fuck that. This was Rafe and Mikey, the only people who'd seen all of her warts and still wanted her.

She couldn't believe how perfectly the three of them were coming together.

She'd traveled here terrified Mikey would see her as a freak. But he'd taken everything in stride the last three days, and not only had he understood, he'd wanted more. He'd wanted her *and* Rafe, which seemed like the solution to all their problems.

The truth was, she hadn't been sure she was ready to move on from Rafe. Despite all he'd said about what he couldn't give her, she felt safe with him. Protected. Not to mention understood. The idea of losing all that, of losing *him*, made her sick to think about. It was part of why she'd been avoiding decisions about her future. Maybe now she wouldn't have to.

She truly cared about both of them, and something was definitely brewing between Mikey and Rafe, so why couldn't the three of them have a relationship that colored outside the lines? Poly-fidelity was a term she'd learned while performing in that play; the idea of being faithful to more than one person, a closed arrangement all parties agreed to. They didn't need to comply with any rules—the Theory of Deviance said so—and they could be living the dream.

They could rent a little cottage somewhere. Mikey could keep playing guitar. They could do summer stock and community theater, filling their days with song and their nights with frantic, sweaty sex.

Krissy twirled around, skipped over to drop onto the futon, and smiled at the ceiling. Was it having sex again or being onstage that was making her feel this good? Her performance had brought on a massive high better than any drug, and now she felt amazing. Invincible. Even her skin was tingling. She'd bet she could fly if she tried. She almost wanted to go to the roof to see if it was possible, then laughed at herself. *That* was crazy, and she wasn't. She was just really happy.

Her phone buzzed in her sweatshirt pocket. When she thumbed over her screen, the euphoria ebbed. Quiet, like the snow outside.

What are you doing up so late?

She could almost hear her big sister's disapproving tone in the text message. The twelve-year age gap between them had Kim acting like another parent growing up, and even more so since Krissy had gotten sick.

I could ask you the same thing, Kimmy.

It was a dare, a goad for her sister to dish some juicy gossip about how blissful her newly married life was. A reply came quickly.

I just finished doing my rounds. Call me.

Of course. Kim was an oncologist in a children's hospital, her husband a respected surgeon. Her late nights were spent saving lives, not fingering herself in between two gorgeous men.

Her loss. Krissy chuckled, thumbed over to her contacts, and tapped on her sister's name. It barely rang once before Kim picked up.

"You didn't answer my question," she said.

"Hello to you too." Krissy sat up and stretched her legs out in a split, leaning toward one pointed toe. "It's not a big deal. It's not that late."

"It's so late, it's early."

"Then I'm getting a jump on tomorrow!"

Krissy brought her nose to her other knee, feeling the burn in her calf as the tension eased. She should take ballet lessons again. She could become a ballerina. Start her own dance troupe.

"Mom called me."

Krissy froze mid-stretch.

"So?" she asked, but her sister's sigh said it all. "I'm on vacation, Kim. And I'm twenty-one. I don't have to check in every single second."

"It's not every single second, it's once a day." The sound of chair wheels screeching against a linoleum floor made Krissy wince. She could see her sister leaning back in her seat, jet-black hair in a perfect bun beneath the hospital's fluorescent lights, white lab coat over her scrubs, a concerned scowl marring her elegant features. "It's what we all agreed to, after what happened."

"After I went crazy, you mean."

She used the word on purpose, even though she wasn't supposed to.

It had been barred from her family's vocabulary when her therapist corralled them into his office a few days after she'd been released from the loony bin and set up her recovery plan. Daily check-ins, that was the deal they'd made. Everyone involved to minimize the chance of another hospitalization. But how long was she going to have to stay on lockdown like this? Didn't they see how hard she was working? She was busting her *ass* to be the person she was before her fall from grace. She'd fucked up, but as Mikey pointed out, it wasn't her fault. When were they going to stop punishing her for it?

"You're not crazy," Kim corrected. "You have an illness. A serious one, that needs to be managed properly."

"How am I not managing it properly?"

"By not making any plans for after college. By spending all your time with your gay roommate. Going off to spend a week with him and some guy you just met—"

"I am making plans!" she hollered, then caught herself and whispered, "I went to a theater today to see about auditioning. And Mikey isn't *some guy*. You met him at your wedding. You said you liked him."

Kim's accusations cut deep—the allegation that Krissy wasn't trying. That what she was doing here was a sign of her symptoms being on the rise again. But that wasn't the case. She was enjoying herself. Having fun. Sure, she'd gotten a little off track, but she could rein it in. She could manage it.

"I did like him, but Krissy..." Kim sighed again, and this one was sadder. Heavier. "Mom and Dad are worried. I'm worried."

"I'm fine," Krissy insisted through clenched teeth.

I'm not *getting sick again.*

"All right." It was a white flag thrown on the battlefield, a stay of execution, until Mom and Dad woke up and sent in the real troops. "Is it nice out there? You're having fun?"

Krissy glanced out at the snowy horizon again. A real answer wasn't what Kim wanted. She wanted lip service, the verbal confirmation that Krissy was okay, proof that she was still the person she used to be.

"It's nice," she responded stiffly. "We ate lobster. It was great."

The shrill sound of Mikey's cell phone ringing interrupted her. Who would be calling him at this time of night?

"I've gotta go." Krissy bolted to her feet and searched for the source of the noise. "Talk to you later."

Kim's goodbye vanished under the sound of another ring. Krissy finally found Mikey's phone on the kitchen table, the word *Dad* on the screen.

Thoughts about horrible emergencies passed through her mind. The call went to voicemail before she had the chance to get Mikey, but it didn't matter because he was racing from the bedroom, bare feet skidding over the floor as he shoved his glasses on. His hair was a mess, his thin, strong body naked except for boxer briefs.

Krissy swallowed down the pulse of desire it shot through her. Now wasn't the time.

"It was your dad," she said.

"Great." Mikey held out his hand. He passed his free one over his forehead as she handed him the phone, dragging back the dark mop falling into his eyes. "Why is it freezing in here?"

Oops.

"The window." She nodded jerkily over her shoulder. "I needed some air."

Frowning at her, he pulled her to the futon, wrapped a blanket around her, then marched to the still-open window. He paused for a second, looking out at the wintery landscape before drawing the glass down and palming his phone. Sighing, he held it to his ear.

"You called?" he asked, then shook his head. "I'm *off* this week, Dad."

His shoulders slumped as he bracketed a hand against the window. Krissy didn't know what was being said on the other line, but Mikey's replies of "Yes, I see the weather" and "Fine. I'll be there soon" were a pretty good clue.

He ended the call and turned around. "I've gotta go."

"Because of the snow?"

Stupid question. But she had to quiet the nasty voice inside her that whispered, no matter how much Mikey's actions had proven the contrary, he was leaving because of her.

"Yeah. It's not a blizzard or anything. Just bad enough that they need my help."

He grabbed the remote, flipped the TV on, and found a local news station. A winter weather warning blared from the red ticker at the bottom of the screen.

"I have to head home to suit up," he said. "I won't be gone long. We should be done before the morning rush hour. What are you doing up, by the way?"

"I couldn't sleep." She put a tentative hand on his arm, circled her thumb and forefinger around his wrist. His hands were lovely, so capable of creating so much music and pleasure. "Is this what you want to be doing?"

Mikey laughed. "Freeze my ass off while I shovel? Not so much."

"No—" She paused. It was no more the time to be asking him things than it was to be getting horny, but now she'd seen the real him. She hated it that he had to go out there and put a mask on, become someone different just to please everybody else. "I mean, who you are for your parents and the people at your church. Is that the version of yourself that you want to be forever?"

It was a loaded question, one with so many layers to it even she couldn't keep track. But she was looking for...something. A confirmation, to see where he stood. To see if the fairy tale she'd fantasized about having with him and Rafe was something he'd be game for too.

"I don't know." Mikey held her gaze for a moment, then rotated his wrist so he was the one holding her hand. He brought her knuckles to his lips for a chaste kiss. "Can we talk about this later? I'm sorry, I've got to shower and get moving."

She smiled, hoping he couldn't see the raw edge of nerves behind it. "Sure."

When he'd finally gone out into the day, cold air rushing inside along with a burst of snowflakes before he shut the steel door behind him, Krissy went to the bedroom and crawled under the covers beside Rafe.

"You okay?" he mumbled. He was facedown, muscular arms hugging the pillow beneath his head.

"I think so," she whispered, tracing the lines of ink on his back.

She knew how much he loved the design. He was proud of the idea that he was a fallen angel, something wicked and rebellious that had been cast out of his family's narrow-minded version of heaven, and wanted that permanently etched on his skin. But Krissy always wondered if a small part of him had done it as a penance—a reminder of the person his parents had seen when they looked at him in the hospital, any good in him forever tinged by the bad.

Sometimes, she didn't feel so different herself.

"You like Mikey, don't you?" she asked.

"Of course I do. I told you that."

"Not just for me. For you too."

He sighed, then slowly turned over, reached up, and touched her temple.

"What's going on in there?" he asked, gazing at her from those soft, dark eyes that, even when he said they couldn't be together, had always felt like home.

"Just thinking this doesn't have to be only a week. The three of us...we could be more."

His lips curled up into a small, sad smile. She loved Rafe, she truly did, but why did he have to look at her the same way her family did?

"Let's not talk about this now," he said. "Come here. You need to sleep."

His response wasn't so different from Mikey's.

Krissy gave in, closing her eyes and sinking onto the mattress as Rafe curled an arm around her. Maybe they were both right. Now wasn't the time to make decisions. She didn't want to deal with reality anyway. She wanted to be here, in the bliss she'd found with the two of them in this quiet corner of the world.

So she burrowed deeper under the covers, letting Rafe shelter her as he always did, and waited for Mikey to return to them.

TEN

Mikey dug his shovel into a pile of white on the sidewalk, secured it there, and stretched. The hind ridge of the storm hugged the water in the distance, sun breaking through at the faint edge where the grey horizon of ocean met the clouds. It was a good thing too, since seven a.m. was approaching.

Exceptional service was the Pelletier Promise, and their customers signed their contracts with the knowledge that their driveways would be clear by the morning commute. Given the quick punch of today's storm, it was no surprise Mikey's father had called him in.

They would've been out earlier—two was the usual time to get started—but the storm had taken everyone by surprise, accumulating more than predicted.

He should've realized it was approaching when he'd left the theater last night. The air had been oppressive, heavy with the kind of cold humidity that came with snow on the coast. Any other day, Mikey would've been watching the Weather Channel and going through inventory to make sure they had enough salt, looking over their client list and planning which route to take. A lifetime working outside meant he'd gotten pretty good at predicting the weather, but he'd been otherwise occupied.

He took in a lungful of cold, clean air, retrieved the shovel, and went back to work, clearing out the sidewalk around one of their customer's side paths. The hushed skittering of wind through the trees was so peaceful, which was funny since quiet winter mornings hadn't been his favorite in the past.

Three of the company trucks had plows on them, and he'd usually rock-paper-scissors with the other employees to at least be on driveways, warm in the cab with a thermos of coffee and music to keep him company. He always felt loneliest during those times when his only company was a shovel or snow-blower, but he'd volunteered today, content to be outside with his thoughts. He'd attacked the ground with gusto, not needing a break at all, and it wasn't the thermals beneath his sturdy Carhartt coveralls keeping him toasty.

It was the memories of last night.

Amazing. That was the only way to describe it. He was no longer a virgin on so many levels, and Mikey felt like a new man.

Last night was the most accepted, the most comfortable with himself and other people he'd ever felt. Not to mention the most pleasure. The urges he'd had for years were sated, his body relaxed in a way it never had been before. And that final time with Krissy bouncing on top of him, Rafe cupping his balls and easing a lube-slicked finger inside him until he found a spot that made Mikey writhe—he didn't care if it was deviant. He'd do anything to have it again.

The concept of deviance had been on his mind when he'd left the warm den of the apartment and gone out into the dark, bitter morning. Deviation wasn't inherently bad. It just meant departing from accepted social standards. Put in that context, it didn't have to equate to something obscene, a monstrous crime he should abhor. It was all up to interpretation.

So was the word abomination. After all, the Bible said eating shellfish was an abomination, but he didn't see everyone in southern Maine boycotting lobster. And Jesus didn't let cultural norms dictate his relationships. He dined with prostitutes and was loved by social outcasts. He looked beyond what society said to do and saw into people's hearts instead.

Maybe Jesus was the original deviant.

Mikey finished the pathway he was working on, feeling for the first time like a bit of a rebel. All his life, he'd never had the courage to do anything defiant. He hadn't been wild like Dean and Connor were—never got detention, never got into fights or slept around without giving a rat's ass. He'd merely sat in their shadows while they were the irresponsible bad boys he never had the guts to be, reaping the rewards of their protection and reckless attitudes.

Now he wanted to be like them. To have sex. Get a tattoo. To misbehave, and fucking *enjoy it*, for once.

The last driveway on their list cleared, Mikey helped the rest of the team pack their equipment into a company truck. He was dropped off at his parents' house shortly after. Dean's pickup was parked on the driveway where he'd left it, his getaway back to Krissy and Rafe clear, but Mikey could see his mother through the living room windows.

She was at the dining room table, her laptop open in front of her, ever-present cup of herbal tea to its side. She did the billing for the business and was no doubt emailing customers about today's work, invoices with the Pelletier Property Services logo still decked out in red and green for the holidays.

He hadn't gotten to greet her when he'd come through earlier, in too much of a rush to change and hit the pavement. He should at least go in and say hi before heading out again.

He opened the door and stomped off his boots on the mat in the entryway. "Hi, Mom."

"Hi, honey. Dad still out there?"

Mikey nodded. His father had radioed in from the other side of town. "A few places got more than South Portland did. He shouldn't be out much longer."

"Great. Thanks for helping today." She put her elbows on the table, threaded her fingers together, and balanced her chin on her entwined hands. "Are you having fun with Krissy? Is her roommate nice?"

Mikey covered his cringe by looking at his feet, pretending to search for more caked-up snow. He'd told his parents about Krissy when Dean arranged the visit. His mother had tried to hide her enthusiasm, and he could see her doing it again now. A part of him wanted to be honest, but what could he possibly say?

Things are going great, Mom! Turns out her roommate is bi too, and we all fucked like rabbits last night.

"I am," he answered. "Having fun."

"Great. Why don't you invite both girls over for dinner?"

He pinched his lips together. "Krissy's roommate is a guy, Mom. His name is Rafe."

Her mouth opened and closed as she blinked away her surprise. "Oh. Okay. Well you're still welcome. We'd love to meet them."

It was the normal response to have. After all, his mother would never think Mikey was doing...what he was doing.

"Thanks for the invite, but I think I'll pass." He paused, needing to give her some kind of explanation. "I don't know if this is serious with Krissy. I'd rather wait until I'm sure, okay?"

She nodded, the prospect of him actually being serious with a woman enough to pacify her. "Sure. No problem."

He left with his stomach in knots. His parents weren't awful. They were good, hard-working people. They just didn't understand. And everything else aside, there was no point in having Krissy over and getting his mother's hopes up. He really *didn't* know if what they had was serious. Her trapeze answer hadn't told him anything, and it wasn't as if the three of them would be doing this forever.

He didn't like the queasy feeling churning through his gut over that.

Finally back at the warehouse, Mikey parked, took the stairs two at a time, and threw the door open.

"You're back!" Krissy was standing at the kitchen sink, the water running, but she sprinted across the room to throw her arms around him. "And you're freezing!"

"It's cold out there." He pulled back to kiss her. There was batter on her nose. "You made pancakes?"

"Rafe and I had breakfast in bed. Would've been more fun if you were here though."

"I thought you'd be sleeping."

He didn't like it, that she'd been up all night, but she waved him off.

"My parents' call this morning nixed any chance of sleep. No biggie." She winked, then flitted back to the kitchen on the balls of her feet. She had so much energy it made him weary just watching her. "There's some batter left for you. I can cook it if you want."

He kicked off his shoes and hung his coat and snow pants, suddenly exhausted. "Thanks, but I need to lie down for a bit first."

She shooed him into the bedroom, saying she'd be done cleaning soon. Mikey went down the hall. Rafe was in the same place he'd been when Mikey left this morning. His brows lifted as he took in Mikey's appearance.

"You look horrible."

Mikey laughed, a hoarse, tired sound. "I'm beat."

Rafe held a hand out, gesturing to the bed. "Well?"

He didn't even hesitate. This was all going to end too soon, and Mikey wanted to soak up every second of it. Already he could feel the clock ticking toward Saturday and their trip home.

Peeling off everything except his thermals, he climbed onto the bed and stretched out next to Rafe. Barely a second passed before the other man was pulling him close, one arm firmly around him, fingers gentle in his hair. Mikey closed his eyes, body wiped but tingling at Rafe's touch.

"Feels good," Mikey mumbled sleepily. "Thank you."

Rafe's chest dipped on a sharp exhalation. It was a sound Mikey couldn't decipher, the day's strain rushing out of him and his muscles going loose as Rafe pressed a kiss to his forehead.

Krissy came in a few minutes later and curled up behind him, reaching around to flatten her palm over Mikey's heart. He sank into the feeling of being surrounded by them, and fell asleep.

* * *

MIKEY STUMBLED out into the living room a few hours later. Krissy and Rafe were lounging on the couch, her watching TV and he, as usual, staring at his phone.

"You waiting on an important email?" Mikey asked. "The president sharing government secrets?"

Rafe glanced up, his cheeks uncharacteristically flushed.

"Just my agent. I got a callback last week, but given how my last few auditions went, her next message might say it's time to find a new day job." He tucked his phone in his pocket and put an arm around Krissy. "You think the roads are okay yet? We're getting some serious cabin fever here, if you're up for heading out again."

Mikey glanced at Krissy. She didn't look as tired as he thought she'd be. Her eyes were bright, both legs bouncing.

"I know how to handle a little snow on the road. Let's go have some fun."

He drove them down to Kennebunkport, showed them the holiday decorations still up in Dock Square and the tourist destination known as the Wedding Cake House.

"It was built in the early eighteen hundreds," he explained as they idled on the curb, taking in the building's gothic architecture, the buttercream yellow paint and white buttresses, snow lacing every surface like icing. "The story is that the original owner was a sea captain and had the house made for his bride to apologize for never taking her on a proper honeymoon, but I'm pretty sure that's made up."

"It's so romantic," Krissy mused as she dropped her head to Rafe's shoulder, one hand reaching over to clasp Mikey's hand.

They meandered farther south along Route One to the Nubble Light. Krissy made Mikey stop in the parking lot, and she climbed over Rafe to open the door. Braving the chilly spray that shot into the air every time the waves crashed, she ran out to the water's edge to get a picture.

They grabbed some take-out at a sub shop on the side of the road before Mikey drove them back north. Munching happily on a haddock sandwich dubbed a Sea Monster, he turned the radio to his favorite country music station.

"Country?" Rafe asked, but it didn't feel like chastisement. "Seriously?"

"I like country," Mikey insisted. "It's soulful."

"It is. Passionate." Krissy dug into the paper bag on her lap and retrieved a handful of french fries before hollering a loud "Yee-haw!"

Mikey snorted with laughter, but Rafe rolled his eyes. "We're going to have to do something about your musical tastes, Mikey."

Something flared in Mikey's gut. When Rafe and Krissy had arrived, the words *we* and *our* had made him burn with jealousy. Now they included him, and that sat right, like a note he'd been trying to play and finally found.

He brushed the feeling aside.

"Last stop." He pulled into the lot of Portland's Ice Arena. Krissy cooed and clapped, brimming over with enthusiasm as they went inside and rented skates. She laced hers up quickly and rushed into the rink, her dance training evident in the way she skillfully took to the ice.

"I haven't done this in years," Rafe said.

"Not a fan of skating?"

"I am, I just never go. Too busy trying to get gigs and doing temp jobs to cover my rent. Inheritances don't last as long as one might think."

Mikey frowned, wanting to hear more, but he didn't know if asking about Rafe's financial state was okay, no matter how intimate they'd been.

"You'd be looking for another roommate then? If Krissy came here?"

Rafe paused, his jaw working. Something like worry flashed in his eyes, but the look disappeared quickly, vanishing beneath his smile.

"I'll put an ad on Craigslist. Should be easy enough to find someone."

They stayed silent as they finished tying on their skates. Once they'd joined Krissy on the ice and began skating around in circles, Mikey asked, "Is your rent expensive?"

"It's New York," Rafe said. "Everything is expensive."

He turned to skate backward, his blades making S-shaped patterns in the ice as he moved ahead of them for a lap.

"To answer your question," Krissy said. "It's twenty-three hundred a month."

Over two grand. Damn. Although, not as bad as he expected. "Do you like it there? Not the apartment. I mean, in New York."

"It can be overwhelming. It's gritty and unforgiving and rough, but I never feel alone."

Her answer struck a chord. *Alone.* Was his worst fear one more thing they shared?

"You wouldn't feel alone here either," he told her, and sweet Lord, the way she looked at him, her cheeks making a heart shape out of her face, eyes shining...

He wanted to put that look on her face every single day, to be the reason for her happiness.

Was this love? It certainly felt like it, and Mikey suddenly saw his future clicking together. Krissy could move here. He could take care of her and have her comfort and humor all the time. He'd have that perfect, normal relationship he'd wanted with a partner who was more than willing to bring another man into their bed once in a while.

And maybe that was something Rafe would be cool with too.

Back at the apartment, Krissy asked if she could run a bath, saying it might help her sleep. Eager to do anything that would help her unwind, Mikey unearthed some bubble bath from Dean's cabinet, leaving once she was soaking in the tub. He found Rafe sprawled out on the bed, phone off for once and on the nightstand.

"What's the deal with your parents?" Rafe asked him. "You never said."

Mikey sat next to him. "They want me to be straight, if I can. They say it'll be easier for me." He glanced away. It was harder to be as honest with Rafe as he had been with Krissy.

"Fuck them," Rafe said. "They don't have any right to make you feel ashamed about who you are."

"They're my family, Rafe."

"Screw family. If I were you, I'd say *fuck you very much* to them and be on my way."

His words were harsh, and so different from Krissy's sympathetic reaction, but Rafe's sentiment felt like protection nonetheless, wings stretching over him in verbal form. It made Mikey think of Rafe's tattoo, and he wondered if Krissy and Rafe had become the proverbial angel and devil on his own shoulders, tempting him in different directions.

Temptation. That was the feeling that made Mikey's entire body tingle when Rafe sat up, hand sliding past Mikey's jaw to wrap around the back of his neck.

"You wouldn't do that, though, would you?" Rafe shook his head and laughed. "You're a regular saint, Mikey."

"I highly doubt that, but thank you."

"You're welcome."

Warm fingers skimmed over his skin, and Mikey couldn't hide his shiver. Rafe's touch fired him up like lightning. He couldn't stop himself, either, from reaching up to encircle Rafe's wrist. Pulling the other man's arm back, Mikey rubbed along the raised skin of Rafe's scar.

I'm sorry, he tried to say with his thumb. *I'm sorry your parents drove you to this.*

Rafe's chest rose and fell with quickening breaths. His throat worked on a swallow, and he studied Mikey for several seconds, the look in his eyes so pained Mikey was worried he'd crossed a line, but then Rafe was kissing him. Sliding his tongue past Mikey's lips. Leaning over him until Mikey was on his back on the bed and the full lengths of their bodies were pressed together, hips grinding.

Mikey broke the kiss long enough to yank off his glasses, then arched up for more. Rafe sucked on his lower lip, his teeth a rough chafe, and Mikey clambered for a breath. He was fully erect already, dick pressing against his zipper.

He slid his hands along the divots above Rafe's waist, and everything got hot, fast. Shirts were pulled off, pants too. Rafe's eyes blazed as he hooked his fingers in Mikey's briefs, yanked them down, and took him into his throat in one smooth swallow.

"Oh shit," Mikey panted. "Shit, *shit*."

Rafe sucked and hummed, hands holding Mikey's hips down as he slid up to the tip, swirled his tongue, and plunged back down. The pleasure was so intense Mikey had to cover his eyes. It didn't feel quite right, doing this without Krissy, but *fuck*, he couldn't stop.

Rafe was talented, his suction mind-blowingly persistent, and soon Mikey was at the brink. "Stop," he said breathlessly, reaching for Rafe. "Want to suck you too."

"Jesus, yes."

A quick change in position had Rafe on his back, his boxers shucked and Mikey hovering over him, so nervous and excited his hands were trembling. He grabbed the lube from the nightstand and placed it on the bed. With one hand wrapped snugly at the base of Rafe's cock, Mikey slid his mouth over the crown and sucked downward until his gag reflex forced him to back off.

Rafe's fingers were soft on the back of Mikey's neck, a tender pet that said *yes, you're doing fine, keep going.*

A few moments of clumsy sucking later and Rafe was cursing and gripping the sheets. Seeing him come apart like that was intoxicating. Mikey pulled back to pop open the lube. He shot a hasty glance over his shoulder, sure Krissy wouldn't mind. Actually, it'd probably turn her on to walk in on this, eager to come in and join them.

Mikey slicked his fingers, keeping his eyes on Rafe as he massaged the other man's balls, then moved lower.

"I have no idea what I'm doing," he admitted on a shaky laugh.

"You've been a natural so—" Rafe inhaled sharply and bit his lip, eyes sinking closed as Mikey's pinky slid past the first tight ring of muscle.

His reaction was the most erotically satisfying thing Mikey had ever seen.

"More," Rafe breathed, and Mikey switched to his middle finger, shimmying it in a little farther. Rafe's mouth dropped open and his cock twitched, so hard Mikey could almost feel the throbbing in his own dick. He moved in again and lapped at Rafe's thick, swollen tip, closing his eyes at the forbidden, tangy taste of precome. Taking down as much glistening flesh as he could, Mikey continued with gentle thrusts of his finger, searching out the spot Rafe had found in him yesterday.

His hand slamming down on the mattress was a sure sign Mikey had found it.

"Christ, Mikey. Get the condoms."

Mikey stopped moving. *That* he wouldn't do without Krissy. And wait a minute. "Didn't you say sex meant commitment for you? That it meant...love?"

Rafe panted, the line between his brows wedged in deep. He licked his lips and rubbed them together.

"Right. My bad. Just got a little carried away."

Mikey's pulse raced, and not in a good way. "I'm sorry. I'm totally ruining the moment here. I just think we're not being fair to Krissy, not including her."

Rafe nodded, a sharp, jittery move. "Absolutely. Let's move this to the bathroom."

"Okay." Mikey inched his finger back until it was free. Rafe sat up, then paused and scrubbed his hands over his face. "You all right?"

"Totally," Rafe said, but his attempt at enthusiasm seemed forced. "Be right there."

Mikey hesitated, then climbed off the bed, put his glasses on, and headed toward the bathroom. It wasn't that he didn't want to fuck Rafe, but wasn't that crossing another line? He had to pass it off as something said in the heat of the moment. Rafe made it clear he wanted Mikey and Krissy together, everything they'd done this week simply a means to that very specific end.

Rafe didn't have *feelings* for him.

Mikey pushed the bathroom door open. Krissy was out of the tub, naked on the bathmat, hair in a messy bun as she toweled her body off. Rivulets of water dripped down her skin, and Mikey rinsed his fingers, then kissed her, his erection pressing at her waist as he leaned down to take her nipple in his mouth.

"Mikey," she whispered. "Yes. Please."

God, this was confusing. He wanted her as much as he wanted Rafe. But those feelings toward him were just sexual. Pure experimentation.

Right?

Rafe came in behind him, a condom in his hand. Krissy's eyes flashed and she sank to her knees. No stage directions were needed when she started stroking both of them, taking them into her mouth one at a time.

Despite the sudden spike of pleasure racing through him, Mikey reached for Rafe, feeling like he should apologize, like he should say *something*, but Rafe's quick, crushing kiss stole his breath. Rafe pulled back without making eye contact, then hauled Krissy up from the bathmat, kissing her with the same hard determination before pressing the condom into Mikey's hand. Bracing himself against the shower door, Rafe bent Krissy in half and guided her mouth back onto him, positioning her for Mikey to take.

She whined around Rafe's cock, her sounds of need coming out as she sucked. Mikey ripped open the wrapper, sheathed himself, and slid inside.

Krissy's moan was a soft, sinful sound, and Rafe cupped the back of her head, tenderly looking down at her. Mikey would have to have been blind to not see something sad in Rafe's eyes, but his synapses began to misfire as he fucked and watched and felt. He didn't know how it was possible for his chest to ache while everything else felt so damn good, but there was nothing he could do, no way to fix whatever mess this had turned into.

So he gave himself over to sensation, the two of them coming together the last thing he saw before his eyes slammed shut.

ELEVEN

Krissy watched the sunrise the next morning from the living room windows, naked except for a blanket wrapped around her. She hadn't been able to sleep again. Maybe all the sex had supercharged her body somehow. It was awesome, not being tired, but if she didn't get a little rest, she'd be a basket case at the karaoke bar tonight.

So she'd crept out of bed and gone through Rafe's things until she found the baggie Merrick had given him. Her usual trigger had faded, replaced by a curiosity to see if smoking pot would feel the same way it had the last time she'd done it. Before she'd mixed it with other drugs and made a shit-ton of bad decisions. That wasn't going to happen now, not with Rafe and Mikey here, so what was the harm in a little weed if it helped her relax?

She stuck her head out the open window, brought the joint to her lips, and lit it. Breathing in deeply, she closed her eyes and inhaled the mix of cold morning air and sweet marijuana burn. She was sick of never allowing herself to do stuff like this. Of the strict parameters she had to keep on her life, every day a jail cell in the form of yoga, phone calls, and apps.

She'd followed her rules yesterday, speaking to her parents at length when Mikey was out shoveling. They hadn't been as mad as she'd expected. Just uber concerned, of course, so she'd given them a play-by-play, minus the orgasms. She logged her moods all day, made sure she took her pill, and did her hour on the mat, even though her head was spinning too much for meditation.

Today was a new day, though. Almost a whole new year, fresh with possibilities. She took several more puffs, closing her eyes and sinking into the lightheadedness it brought on. One joint wasn't going to kill her. She'd go back to well-behaved Krissy tomorrow.

"What are you doing out here?"

Krissy tossed the joint out the window, hiding the evidence of her indiscretion before Mikey could see it. "Getting my yoga out of the way and greeting the day," she lied, turning around with a smile. "There's no better time to do a sun salutation than at sunrise."

"Krissy!" He crossed the room and bundled the blanket more firmly around her. "You're naked under there."

"So?" She quirked an eyebrow and nodded at the window. "Worried someone will see me?"

She was purposely stoking the flames. Stimulating his voyeuristic tendencies.

"No, I'm worried you'll get sick. Your skin is like ice."

He led her to the futon, wrapped one arm around her, and tried to warm her with the other.

"You make me feel like a kitten." She nuzzled him and broke into giggles over her attempt to purr.

Mikey pulled back, his brow creased. "Are you...okay?"

Oh, man. Now he was looking at her like that too? She lolled her head back against the couch. "I'm fine."

"You're sure?"

A small, uneasy voice inside her whispered "maybe I'm not",

but Krissy ignored it, letting herself sink into the floaty, fuzzy feeling of being high instead. Maybe she was a little *up*, but she'd been taking her meds. If she'd ditched them entirely, that would be different. But nothing was happening, other than the vacation and the pot and the fact that all this awesome stuff was going on.

"I'm sure. Just excited for tonight."

Mikey leaned in and kissed her, all stubble and warmth and morning breath, and she couldn't have cared less. "Okay. I trust you."

He trusted her, had faith in her. Krissy melted, her limbs going slack as she cuddled closer.

"I'm looking forward to tonight too," he added. "Last New Year's Eve totally blew."

"What did you do?"

"Acted as designated while Dean, Connor, and Jamie got wasted. Connor hadn't met Gabriella yet and almost got into a fight at the bar we went to. Dean disappeared with some girl because he still had his head up his ass about Jamie, and Jamie almost gave me a heart attack when she pretended she'd covered the inside of Dean's truck with silly string."

It was a funny story, but it didn't quite gel with the people she'd met. Krissy had spent a limited amount of time with Mikey's friends back in the fall. She'd enjoyed their stories of being a ragtag bunch of teenagers but hadn't seen any evidence of it.

"They seem like they've got their stuff together now."

"It's pretty recent. Most of our lives, they were the wild ones while I was tagging along, never quite fitting in."

Krissy reached up and stroked his hair. The locks fell across his forehead in haphazard waves. He might have thought he wasn't a rebel, but look at what he'd done in the last few days. Sure, it was behind closed doors, but he wasn't obeying any rules or accepting normal standards of behavior.

"I think you're pretty wild," she said. "You were definitely wild last night."

He blushed, and Krissy's own cheeks heated at the memory. The way he and Rafe came into the bathroom together was hot as hell. She'd loved the daisy chain they made: Rafe in her mouth, Mikey slamming into her from behind. He'd taken her with a ferocity she hadn't expected from someone who'd been a virgin just a few days before, leaving her pleasantly sore afterward, but once it was over, she wanted more.

She'd hoped Rafe would take her too.

Being with Mikey had reminded her how much she'd missed that link. Yes, she loved being touched, but there was a different kind of connection when someone was inside her, an intimacy that couldn't be established with hands alone, and she'd wanted to share that with Rafe as well.

Maybe it couldn't happen yesterday, but that might change, because there'd been a new element to everything last night. A fresh passion that suddenly sparked. She'd seen it in the way Rafe kissed Mikey. It was a more intense kiss than they'd had before. He'd kissed her with the same deep passion, like he was trying to tell her something. Like even though he hadn't wanted to discuss it yesterday, he'd realized the three of them belonged together.

It wasn't the high, or her bipolar talking. She should've trusted her emotions from the start. She was in love with Mikey, and who was she kidding? She'd always loved Rafe. She knew Mikey didn't want to be the person his parents were forcing him to be, and Rafe had only said he hadn't want to talk about it, not that the three of them couldn't work.

Because they could. They totally could.

Reality could be as good as the fantasy they'd shared. And it was going to be amazing.

The floor creaked behind them, and Rafe came into the living room. Krissy arched back to greet him, but he was frowning at his phone. Whatever he was reading, it was apparently a long message, and the line that had formed between his eyebrows got her worrying it was his agent, breaking their contract.

"Bad news?" she asked.

A minute passed before he answered. It was actually a minute too. She counted. When he finally glanced up, she swore a shadow passed over his face, but he threw on one of his signature casual grins.

"Nope. Just more of the same. You kids excited for tonight?"

Whew. Krissy knew Rafe's savings were on the cusp of drying up. He needed whatever show his agent could land him. A short stint would be better, though. A limited run, so they could move here after her graduation.

She punched a fist in the air. "New Year's Eve, here we come."

* * *

THEY WERE out the door by nine that evening, Krissy in a short black dress with a flouncy waist and Converse sneakers, her hair pulled into a sleek ponytail. Rafe wore slacks and a crisp white shirt, and Mikey was in black jeans, a button-down, and a silver tie. Krissy's head was buzzing with that *am-I-really-here* feeling she had when she was overtired, but the party would snap her out of it. She'd tried to nap a couple of times, finally giving up when the sun dipped below the horizon. She'd chosen to dance around the apartment and blast music instead. She needed to warm up her voice if she was going to sing tonight, and hoped her antics would get Mikey and Rafe out of the funk they both seemed to be in.

Whatever. If she couldn't party it out of them, she'd fuck it out of them later.

The dive bar they were meeting Merrick at was packed to the

brim. It barely fit a hundred, lousy acoustics making the room even louder from all the people talking and laughing. Multicolored lights turned the dance floor into an inferno of color. A disco ball hung from the ceiling, and a small stage in the corner was set up with a screen. Merrick ran over to greet them and grasped Krissy's hand.

"You're singing again, baby," he said.

He cued up the karaoke machine to Prince's "1999". Krissy belted out the lyrics, the anxiety that used to plague her now a thing of the past. The evening passed in a flurry of music and dancing and a tiny bit of champagne. Mikey stayed sober since he was driving, but Rafe was back to his jovial self after a pre-midnight toast and a couple of shots. A little before twelve, he donned one of the plastic, gold, sparkly top hats the bartender had handed out and joined Merrick in a duet of George Michael's "Faith".

Krissy and Mikey watched from the dance floor, his arms around her with her back to his chest, both of them cheering as Rafe and Merrick played at grinding on the stage. Not touching, just pretending, showing off for them. Krissy reached up behind her to slide a palm along Mikey's cheek.

These boys. These boys and her. God, she'd never been so happy. She was swinging on that trapeze again, jumping happily from one of them to the other. She went up on her tiptoes and tilted her head back until her lips met his ear.

"I love our little secret," she said.

"What secret?"

"This. Us. You, me, and Rafe." Krissy spun around until she was facing him. Her heart pounded, her hands shook. She didn't need drugs. She was high on this fucking brilliant idea. "I have something to tell you."

His smile was better than fireworks. "What's that?"

"After I graduate, Rafe and I should move here."

She pivoted around, trying to dance with him, but he'd gone stiff. "Both of you?"

"Wouldn't it be awesome?" Her voice was only high and squeaky because of the noise in here. She *had* to be loud, so he could hear. "We'll all live together. Think how incredible that'll be."

He wasn't dancing. Why wasn't he dancing? She went on her tiptoes and threw her arms around him.

"This doesn't have to stop at the end of the week. Why should it? We're having way too much fun. He and I could come here, the three of us could be a triad. No, a trifecta, because we're that perfect. Like the three witches, the three fates. The holy trinity, or mind, body, and soul."

Mikey put his hands on her arms and gently disentangled her. Around them, the music had stopped and people were counting.

"Krissy, people don't actually do that."

"Sure they do. Haven't you ever heard of a poly-fidelitous relationship? It's totally a thing."

The counting was getting louder. And Mikey was no longer smiling. "Look, I know this has been fun but, the three of us together, here—" he swallowed, "—that's not very realistic."

There it was again. That *look* in his eyes.

I'm not crazy. I'm not crazy.

"You said I wouldn't be alone here!"

"I said *you*, not...both of you."

"So what has this week been? I saw you with Rafe. You want him too."

He winced. "Maybe, but I can't do...that."

"Can't, or won't?"

It didn't matter. She'd read him all wrong. Maybe she wasn't being fair, but she'd thought he was different, thought he wouldn't judge her, and she couldn't concentrate anymore because everyone was cheering and confetti was flying everywhere. It was too loud, everything around her a chaotic mix of sound, colors, and light. There were too many people, too much noise. She spun around, searching for Rafe. He wasn't by the microphones.

"Where's Rafe?"

"Wait, Krissy—" Mikey tried to take her hand, but she wrenched away from him and marched through the crowd. Thinking maybe Rafe had gone out for some air, she pushed through the sea of people and went outside.

His gold, plastic top hat sat on the concrete.

Mikey was right behind her. "Krissy, hold on a—"

"Leave me alone," she snapped. Her fingers were going numb as she fumbled through her wristlet for her phone.

You haven't logged your mood yet. How are you feeling right now?

"Shut up!" she yelled at the screen, swiping past it to the text message from Rafe, hoping it said where to find him.

I'm with Merrick. Enjoy your time with Mikey. You two are perfect and should have the night alone together. Happy New Year, sweetheart.

"No!"

She dialed his number immediately, ready to scream at him to come back, to tell him this wasn't what she wanted, but the call went straight to voicemail.

Krissy sank to the curb. A sob ripped from her lungs. "He's gone."

"What do you mean, gone?"

"He left. With Merrick."

Krissy wrapped her arms around her body. Her chest was caving in. She couldn't remember where she'd put her jacket, and her teeth were starting to chatter.

Mikey cursed quietly, then put one hand on her bare arm. "Come on. Let's go. It's cold."

Standing slowly, she followed him robotically inside to get her coat, then back out to the truck. Sitting in the cab, she caught her reflection in the passenger side mirror. Blonde streaks, purple eyes, mascara all over her face. Who *was* this person?

Whoever she was, she looked like hell. And Mikey was seeing it. And Rafe had ditched her with nothing more than a text.

It was a shitty thing to do, but maybe she deserved it. She'd wanted too much, had stretched them all too thin. It was right that he was moving on without her. And as for Mikey, it looked like this had just been about fun for him. She'd been nothing but a gateway drug, a way for him to get a taste of a life he was too scared to actually have.

He slid into the driver's seat. "Is there anything I can do?"

His words had an echo to them, like they were coming from a long way off. She'd been here before—this dark place she was sinking into was sickeningly familiar, but finding her way out of it was like scratching at the side of a smooth, damp wall. All she wanted to do was close her eyes. Even responding to Mikey was too much effort.

When she didn't answer, he drove them back to the apartment. She went straight to the bedroom and crawled under the covers, her clothes still on.

"Will you at least take your shoes off?"

"No." It was the longest word she could manage. She was humiliated. Disgraced by what she'd done with him, by how much she'd opened up. How much of a fool she'd been.

He sighed quietly. "You need to take your meds."

She didn't move. The bed shifted beside her and she heard sounds—a pill container unscrewing. A water bottle top coming off.

"Krissy," he said, a little more forcefully. "Please sit up and take your pill."

She snapped upright, snatched the pill from his hand, and swallowed it dry before diving back under the covers. The silence stretched on until Mikey sighed again and stood.

"I'll let you rest. I'll be in the living room if you need me."

She didn't answer. She knew she was being horrible. She was too numb to care. The hole she'd fallen into was too deep for her to feel anything but pain. All she wanted was oblivion.

He left the room, and Krissy stared into the darkness until the black emptiness of sleep found her.

TWELVE

"**R**afe, pick up your damn phone!"

Mikey yelled the same message he'd left five times into Rafe's voicemail, then ended the call and dropped his phone on the couch. He'd copied Rafe's number from Krissy's contacts and tried him a dozen times over the course of the night, nodding off in between calls and jumping up to check on her. She hadn't moved, hadn't spoken to him once. Now it was morning, and the silence he was getting from both of them was deafening.

He needed to find Rafe, right the fuck now.

Moving into the bedroom, he stood by the side of the bed and spoke quietly. "I need to run out for a bit. You'll be safe here, and I'll have my phone on me the whole time. Call me right away if you need anything, okay?"

She didn't answer.

Not that he blamed her. He'd watch the light in her eyes go out when he shot her down last night. It had killed him to say so, but she had to know there was no way he could live here with them in some kind of poly triad. He figured she'd be upset but *this*...this was terrifying.

He had no idea how far her sudden depression could go or how long it would last, and had spent some time during the night looking up hotline numbers and reading about bipolar lows. He hadn't wanted to leave her alone, but she wouldn't fucking *talk* to him, and getting Rafe back seemed like the best course of action.

Bundling up, Mikey went downstairs and slammed the truck door shut. He'd never been so mad. How could Rafe go off and leave them like that? Did he care so little about Krissy?

Did Rafe care so little about him?

It was an unfair thought to have. He knew Rafe was hurt. The cavern that had opened between them yesterday was proof of that. But abandoning them without a word, going off with Merrick...it made Mikey sick. And the thought of Rafe being touched by someone other than him or Krissy, he couldn't stand it.

Mikey gripped the steering wheel, unable to move. He closed his eyes and prayed for a way to fix this, but given the circumstances, was God really going to answer?

His phone beeped with a text. Mikey snatched it from his pocket.

You're supposed to be with Krissy.

Rafe. Mikey pressed the heel of his hand against his temple in relief, then shoved his hair out of his eyes.

Where are you? he typed back. Then, nauseously, *Are you still with Merrick?*

Like that was ever going to happen.

What the—

Don't worry about me, the next text said. *Be with Krissy. I'm fine.*

Bullshit. *Where the hell are you?*

No reply.

Mikey banged his head against the seat in frustration. Why was Rafe doing this? If he wasn't with Merrick, then he was off alone somewhere, feeling like he wasn't welcome. If Mikey were in Rafe's place, where would he go?

Where had he gone when he was running away from them?

Mikey threw his phone on the seat and put the truck in drive.

A few minutes later he pulled up in front of his church. Rafe was huddled on the steps with his head bowed. Mikey cut the engine and marched to Rafe's side. He had half a mind to yank him up and drag him back to the apartment without saying a word, but the guy looked like a ghost, sitting by himself on those bleak cement stairs.

"What are you doing?" Mikey asked.

Rafe raised his head. His tear-streaked face didn't match his wry smile. "Asking for forgiveness."

"For what?"

Rafe's shoulders shook on his chuckle. "For being selfish. What else?"

Mikey sat next to him. The concrete was freezing. "How long have you been here?"

"A while. I had Merrick drop me off." He studied the ground in front of him. "We didn't do anything, just so you know. I tried, but I couldn't. He's not who I want."

Something wrenched through Mikey—feelings of hope and confusion and worry that were too many layers of complicated for words. "Am I?"

Rafe looked away.

"Was that your fantasy then?" Mikey asked. He and Krissy had dished their darkest desires, but Rafe had never mentioned his. "This is all because you wanted sex with me?"

A short, sharp laugh escaped him. "No. That's not my fantasy."

"What is it then?"

"Unconditional love."

His answer was a sucker punch to Mikey's gut. The idea that love was such a far-off thing for Rafe he considered it a fantasy? How was that possible?

"I get it now," Rafe said quietly. "Why Krissy fell for you so fast. I thought it was her being too emotional. But I understand, because I did the same thing." He shook his head—at the irony of it all, Mikey supposed. "You're so good. So damn open and honest. You're everything I'm not and everything I wish I could be."

Mikey had to wince at the awful twist of fate. Wasn't that what he'd thought of Rafe when he'd first seen him?

Rafe sighed heavily. "I knew it was time to remove myself from the picture when I realized I had feelings for you. Krissy cares about you so much. I couldn't do that to her."

Mikey's lungs went tight, his heart tripping over the knowledge that Rafe felt that way, his chest constricting with all that implied.

"It doesn't make what you did last night okay."

Rafe laughed again, and the wild, abrupt noise came out sounding a little mad. "I know. See? My parents were right. I am a selfish prick."

"No you're not."

"I am. I'm the most selfish person in the world, because what I really want is both of you."

"Wait, what?"

Nothing was making sense, until it suddenly did, Rafe looking up at him like his heart was breaking.

"I lied," he said on a shrug. "I kept sex off the table with Krissy because I don't want to hurt her, not because I don't love her. You have no idea how many times I've had to stop myself from going into her room and giving her what we've both wanted."

Despite how messed-up everything had become and how damn *cold* Mikey was, the picture of the two of them together like that made him flush with warmth.

Still, Rafe had been lying to her. Lying to him.

"So, the stuff about just falling for men—that was all garbage?"

"No, that part's true, mostly. I've only been in love with men in the past. And I can care about more than one person at a time. That much is—" he waved a hand in Mikey's direction, his voice breaking on the word, "—obvious. But Krissy and I aren't good together. We're too alike. Too emotional, too impulsive. When we want something, we want it intensely. This week is a perfect example. I wanted her to fall in love, and look what happened."

Mikey thought about the panic in Krissy's eyes when she saw Rafe's text. The way she'd looked at Rafe when they arrived at the train station.

"I think she's already in love, Rafe."

Rafe took a deep, shuddery breath and stared up at the sky.

"What the hell do I know about being worthy of someone's love? All I've ever known of love has ripped my heart out." He pulled his knees into his chest and wrapped his arms around them. He looked so small and sad, and Mikey finally saw how hurt Rafe had been. How heartbroken he still was.

Rafe balanced his chin on his knee, then turned his head toward Mikey and smiled.

"I'm in awe of your ability to forgive, Mikey. It's what I really like about you. And being with you both this week, it's everything I could ever want, but I'm not good for you. For either of you. *You're* right for her. You're stable and strong. You're not damaged like I am. And Krissy will never let me go until she sees that." Rafe's face hardened again. He looked back at the ground. "That's why I left with Merrick. If I hurt her before I leave, she won't be thinking about me when I go."

Mikey froze, and not from the cold. "You're leaving?"

"I got a job. A part in a national touring company. Email came in from my agent yesterday."

The impact of Rafe's statement hit him head-on. Mikey stared at him in horror. "How long will you be gone?"

"Nine months. Gotta be packed by Sunday."

"You can't do that to her! As it is, she's practically falling apart."

Rafe stiffened. "What do you mean?"

"She hasn't said a word since you took off. I was ready to call an ambulance. I was scared to death to leave her alone, but I did it to find you."

Rafe lowered his head, but Mikey wasn't interested in giving the guy pity. No matter how he felt about Rafe—yes, he had to admit there were feelings there, feelings he couldn't sort out yet—he'd have to deal with that later.

"I'm not going to let you break her like that, Rafe. She might never recover. You might think it's the right thing to do, but you're wrong. Maybe she needs someone like me in her life, but she needs you too. So get your ass in that truck."

The aggressive sound of his own voice surprised Mikey, but he'd yell if that's what it took to get Rafe moving.

He stood and walked down the steps. Rafe followed, his posture tense. When they arrived at the apartment, Rafe walked ahead of Mikey and into the bedroom. Krissy sat up when she saw him and started to sob.

"I'm sorry." Rafe rushed to her side and pulled her into his arms. "I'm so sorry."

He tucked Krissy's head under his chin, and Mikey stood back as they held each other and cried. He wasn't jealous. If anything, he felt like he could finally breathe again. Krissy looked at him, and her big, watery eyes were filled with gratefulness, uncertainty, and regret.

Mikey shook his head. Now that they were both warm, safe, and together, he needed to make some sense of his own thoughts.

"You two talk," he said. "I'll be back later."

Outside and on the pavement, Mikey dug his hands in his jacket pockets and walked until he reached the harbor's edge. The morning sky was a wash of oranges and reds. Untouched piles of snow were golden where the sunlight hit them, the surface tinted with purplish blue shadows. Mini icebergs bobbed on the waves, the ocean crisp and blue.

Sitting down on a rock, Mikey pulled out his phone and thumbed through messages he hadn't gotten to read in last night's chaos. Connor wishing him a happy new year, saying he and Gabby would be home soon. Dean hoping Mikey made good use of his bed, a wink emoticon after a reminder to wash the linens.

That was friendship—his buddies still looking out for him across state borders. But Mikey had never been himself with them, never been able to tell them the truth.

The only people he'd done that with were Krissy and Rafe.

It made perfect sense that Rafe loved Krissy. It was evident in all the ways he cared for and protected her. In how he'd brought her here, hoping she'd find the kind of security he felt he couldn't offer her.

Mikey thought about Rafe sitting outside alone, wanting both him and Krissy but feeling undeserving of their attention. Rafe talked a good story about not needing family, not compromising himself for anyone and being content with who he was, when the truth was his parents had robbed him of so much affection he was starved for it. It was why he hid his accent, wanting to banish any version of his former self, casting out the person his family had exiled.

He seemed so confident, so charming and charismatic, but that was all a mask. On the inside he was like the Wizard of Oz behind the magic. A little boy desperate for love.

And then there was Krissy. She thought she was too much of a mess for a real relationship, so she'd holed herself up in half of one, afraid to let anyone else in. Mikey had seen her as this shining star, this bundle of energy and cheer, when she was more like him than he'd ever realized.

Just like him, she was punishing herself for what she perceived as a former infraction, not allowing herself to open up. Working herself to the bone to be the person she thought she had to be for her family instead of doing what was right for her. And when she'd figured out what was right, even had the courage to suggest it to him, all Mikey had done was kick her in the teeth for it.

He cared for them both. Deeply. But where did he go with these feelings? Choosing one of them over the other made his heart hurt. He wished he could be with both of them, but how? What would happen to the community he'd made for himself? Would his parents ever forgive him?

He glanced left, toward his church's spire in the distance.

What would God think?

He thought back to Krissy's question from the other day—if he wanted to keep doing what he was doing. He didn't *dislike* working for his folks. There was a great deal of satisfaction to be found in working the land, in seeing the fruits of his labors in summer, in how caring for the ground properly in winter ensured nature's comeback in spring. But he didn't love it, and couldn't truly love the church job either, not with the beliefs he'd grown up with and his parents' fears hanging over him.

He still wanted to do something where he felt he was serving God, but the life he'd been living was suffocating him. Like ivy had grown over him without him realizing it, a darkness he hadn't noticed until Krissy and Rafe broke through and brought in the light.

He looked across the water to the wharf. To Portland, his

home. He *knew* this place. Knew the tides by the scent of the air. Knew when the first frost was coming and when the last one was firmly behind them. He knew his church too, but that didn't mean this was where he belonged.

All his life, he'd felt like the ugly duckling, unwanted because he was different. He thought he needed to change to fit in, when he'd really never been ugly. He just hadn't found his flock of swans yet.

Now he had, and he wanted to be with them. Krissy needed two trapezes to swing from, two people to catch her in case she fell, and Rafe was so broken by his past that he needed more than one person's love to heal him.

Mikey could be what they needed. He had the stuff to take care of them both, and they'd never let him feel alone. They made him whole in a way he'd never imagined, and the sexual gratification in being with them, in *watching* them, had turned him on in ways he couldn't ever have conceived.

He needed to step in, because the two of them were going to fall apart without him.

No side of the triangle was right by itself—the emotional balance only worked when they were together. He wanted to be the glue that kept the three of them whole more than anything, even if it meant deviating from the norm. Even if it meant living a life he wasn't sure fit into the Bible. Even if it meant leaving home.

For years he'd been trapped in his own personal purgatory, worried God wouldn't accept him, hoping he'd find the right person to help him change. But he had found the right person. Two of them. And maybe, God had sent them to him.

He could be a good Christian and love more than one person. God loved everyone, and no one ever got down on Him for that.

Mikey looked at the sky and smiled. Sitting there at the cusp of a new year, the foggy and amorphous desires he'd been agonizing over finally crystallized into something clear. The solution was simple. But he needed to have a conversation first. He needed to sort out his own life before he could offer anything to Krissy and Rafe.

He closed his fingers around the keys in his pocket and walked quickly back to Dean's truck.

THIRTEEN

Krissy took a steadying breath, all her tears washed out of her like a storm that had moved on in the distance. Her eyes were scratchy, her lenses so blurred she could hardly see, and Rafe's shirt was soaked through.

"I'm still mad at you for leaving," she told him.

"That's okay," he said on a sigh. "I'm mad at me too."

He'd apologized a dozen times, saying he'd thought it was the right thing to do. That he should've realized how disappearing like that would affect her. Rafe squeezed her tightly.

"Can you be mad at me and still forgive me?" he asked.

Krissy pressed her forehead to his chest. "Yes."

She wasn't really mad—she was more hurt than anything else, and in mourning for the threesome that could've been. Things wouldn't have turned out this way if Rafe hadn't run off, but then again, how long had she been relying on him, using him as a human safety net?

Too long.

Krissy sat up and listened for the sounds of Mikey in the

apartment. The place was as silent as it had been since he'd left an hour ago, and that wasn't because of Rafe. That was all her.

What a mess she'd made of things. Mikey probably hated her now. She put her head in her hands. Everything hurt—her fingers, her skull.

Her heart.

"I smoked your other joint yesterday," she said.

"I know. I saw the empty bag."

"And you didn't say something?"

"I guess I thought it wasn't my place anymore."

"Why?"

Rafe sat up slowly, his shoulders hunched, brows drawn tight. "I got a show, Krissy. A national tour. Rehearsals start in Milwaukee on Monday."

Her stomach dropped. "You're leaving me?"

"I need this show, Kris. And me going means you and Mikey can make things work."

She snorted. "I doubt Mikey wants anything to do with me."

"I know for a fact that isn't true."

Didn't matter. He and Krissy wouldn't work right on their own, not after everything the three of them had shared.

"And what about you?" she asked. "Who should you be with?"

He smiled sadly. "No matter who chooses who, somebody gets hurt. Might as well be me."

"I'm not okay with you sacrificing yourself. I don't want you to be hurt. I don't want anyone to be hurt."

The silence grew heavy. Rafe touched her arm. "Kris, I—"

"Please don't say it." She knew what was coming next wasn't another apology. They'd exhausted those when they were crying. There were no more sorrys left between them. "Please don't say goodbye."

"It's not goodbye. It's…" He winced. "I've been holding you back, being with you like we have. It seems like I've been taking care of you, but really I've stopped you from moving forward."

She inhaled a shuddery breath. There was truth to what he was saying, but the words were another stab at her already bruised heart.

"When do I need to be out of the apartment?" she asked.

"You don't. It's yours. Hell, have Mikey move in with you. But I need you to take better care of yourself. You've been acting like you are, but I can see through it. I know you, and you're not okay." He cupped her face, forcing her to meet his gaze. "Please, *please*, promise me you're going to do something about that."

She nodded, feeling her face crumple. "I'll try."

"Okay. I have to go home tomorrow instead of Saturday. I already switched my train ticket. I left a message for Dean and Jamie. Told them I wouldn't get in the way, just have to come through to grab my things." He pressed his lips to her forehead and held still for a long moment before pulling away. "I need to shower and pack."

It was all Krissy could do to stay upright as he went into the bathroom. She wanted to dive under the covers, to crawl into a cave of blankets and never come out. But she couldn't let herself, because through the hazy fog of her pain, she recognized what was happening. It wasn't just Rafe leaving or Mikey crushing her dream.

She'd fallen into a cycle without realizing it.

It had been coming on for a while, probably starting back when she'd changed her hair. She should've recognized the signs, but she'd been too caught up in finals, the holidays, and preparing for this trip.

She'd been on an upswing this whole week, could even track it if she looked at her mood app. The mania had pushed through her meds. A crash was inevitable, and smoking pot yesterday morning, followed by everything else that happened, had sent her careening into a low.

There was one thing she was sure about though. One thing that didn't have her wondering if it was the bipolar or her: her love for Rafe and Mikey. That was real. And so was what they did for one another. Rafe revved her up while Mikey calmed her. One sheltered, the other encouraged. All their kinks matched up, their emotions too, but Rafe was right, and the looks Mikey had been giving her yesterday were right too.

She wasn't taking care of herself. She'd been pretending she was fine when she wasn't. Hiding behind Rafe, behind her wild clothes. Behind streaked hair and colored contacts, the word crazy, and the curtain of the stage. Maybe that's why she loved the theater—because it was such an awesome place to hide.

It was time to stop hiding.

Krissy stood and went to her bag. As much as she hated it, she knew she couldn't hang onto things with Rafe, and she didn't want to expect anything from Mikey either. His rejection was a raw nerve that hadn't been soothed. But even if the three of them somehow found their way back to one another, she needed to be whole for herself first. She needed to accept that she wasn't going to be normal again—not the way she used to be—and find a better way to manage her illness on her own.

To learn how to catch herself when she was between trapeze rungs, even if Rafe and Mikey were the ones who made her soar.

Pulling what she'd been looking for from her duffle, she went to the bedroom mirror. One by one, she took out her contacts and dumped them in the trash, then put on her glasses. She looked at her reflection, and saw herself clearly for the first time in a while. Then she picked up her phone and dialed, closing her eyes as it rang.

"Mom?" Her voice was cracking. She didn't want to admit this, but... "I don't think my meds are working. I need to go back to the doctor again."

* * *

AN HOUR LATER, the plans had been made. It was like falling down in an avalanche, telling her parents she needed help, but they'd been great about it, promising to give her all the support she needed instead of the disappointment Krissy had feared. She'd changed her ticket too after that, planning to go home to Connecticut for a while. Once she'd filled Rafe in on everything, she changed out of her dress into some comfy sweats and started to pack.

They were both nearly finished when she heard front door opening. Mikey stepped cautiously into the bedroom. He paled when he saw their bags.

"You're leaving?" he asked.

"I'm heading back early," Rafe answered. "Gotta be ready for that show."

Mikey glanced at Krissy. "You're going too?"

"I'm going home to my folks. Maybe taking some time off school." She tangled her hands in her sweatshirt sleeves. It still stung, remembering how disgusted he'd seemed by her plan, but expecting him to jump on board hadn't been reasonable, given his family and his beliefs. "I haven't been all that healthy. It's probably why I came up with that idea."

Mikey's pallor went a bit chalky. "So you don't want to move here?"

"I don't know yet. I need to take better care of me before I make any other plans."

"What about your apartment?"

"I want Krissy to have it," Rafe said. "I'll look for another place when the tour is over."

Krissy shook her head. "We'll have to sublet until the lease ends. I can't afford it on my own, and my parents aren't going to pay rent for a place I'm not living in."

Mikey nodded. Slowly, very slowly, he treaded toward them. "How would you feel about...subletting it to me?"

Krissy's breath caught. "What?"

He shrugged. "What have I been saving my money for if not to use it on the people I love?"

Love? People?

Krissy threw him a wary glance. "I thought you said you couldn't do this."

"I said I couldn't do it *here*." He took another step forward. "My parents' views might be wrong, but they're still my parents, and I don't want to hurt them. But this place doesn't feel like home anymore. Maybe it never did. The only place that's felt like home is with the two of you."

He held an open palm out toward Krissy.

"You were right," he said. "You knew what I needed all along. I should've trusted you."

Her heart was pounding. She let her fingertips brush along his. "What about the church? And your job?"

"I'll get another one. I've saved enough to keep me afloat for a while. I told my parents I was sorry about the business, but if I can't be me here then it's time for me to go. And there are other churches that might be more—" he grinned, "—forward thinking."

A sheepish smile made its way over her lips. "Last night didn't scare you off?"

"It *scared* me, but it didn't scare me off."

She curled her fingers around his and held her breath as he turned to Rafe. Putting one hand on Rafe's shoulder, Mikey gripped it tightly, his jaw firm as he gave hard looks to both of them.

"So you go home, and get better," he said to her, then looked to Rafe. "And you go on that tour. And when you're both ready, I'll be waiting for you." He shook his head and laughed. "I don't know if this is nuts, but I don't really care. Because no one has made me happier than the two of you have, and I'll do whatever it takes to keep us together."

Krissy couldn't hold back. She buried herself against Mikey's side and grasped Rafe's hand.

"I need to get my head on straight first," she said.

"I know," Mikey said against her hair, putting his arm around her. "I like you with your glasses back, by the way."

A sound that was half a sob, half a giggle burst out of her. Rafe was still holding back though, a bit of distance between him and them.

"You sure about this?" he asked Mikey.

"I'm sure. I'm not walking away from you. I've made my peace with my parents. The rest..." Mikey looked skyward and shrugged. "The rest I'll work out as we go."

Rafe swallowed and looked at Krissy. The piece deep inside her that ached when he said he could never be with her for real wrenched its way to the surface.

Preparing herself for the same answer, she asked him, "Are *you* sure about *me*?"

He took in a shaky breath. "I've always loved you, Kris. I just thought you deserved someone who wasn't so screwed up inside."

Tears welled in her eyes even as her stomach tightened in frustration. He'd been keeping the truth from her for so long, still trying to protect her even at the expense of his own happiness, but it didn't matter. They had something even more beautiful now.

"Well, you're stupid," she told him, and the tension in the room broke on their laughter.

"I'll be gone a long time," Rafe said. "You both sure you want to wait?"

Mikey moved his hand from Rafe's shoulder to grasp the back of his neck. "I've waited my whole life for the two of you. A few more months won't kill me."

Rafe exhaled hard and hung his head. When he lifted it, his eyes were shining. A tear streaked down his face, and Krissy's chest threatened to split in half when Mikey smoothed his thumb over Rafe's cheek, wiping the tear away. He pulled Rafe closer, and Krissy held Mikey tightly as the two of them shared a brief, sweet kiss. It was stunning, witnessing them together, and her breathing quickened when Mikey turned to her and captured her mouth with his.

"You're both leaving tonight?" he asked, his voice husky.

"Not till the morning," Rafe answered. "Why? What did you have in mind?"

Mikey smiled—a scheming one that got Krissy's toes tingling. "One more fantasy."

"Whose fantasy?" she asked.

"All of ours."

He stroked down her arm, clasping her hand once again as he used the other to pin Rafe to the wall. Mikey kissed him, no longer sweet but full of rough passion, then cupped Rafe's face and turned him so he was looking at Krissy.

"Tell her what you've wanted," Mikey murmured.

Rafe's chest heaved. His eyes darkened. He reached for Krissy, slipping out of Mikey's grasp to pick her up. Joy bubbled inside her when he wrapped her legs around his waist and pressed her back to the wall.

"Always," he said, grinding against her. "Always wanted this."

She exhaled on a sigh. Rafe took advantage of her open

mouth and kissed her, sending a tremor down her spine. When he pulled back, Mikey's heavy-lidded expression was pure sin.

"And I want to watch," he said. "To start, anyway."

Krissy felt splotches of heat on her cheeks. Mikey crossed his arms and quirked an eyebrow. "Don't you blush. You're the one who brought this out in me."

Her hips bucked of their own volition. He and Rafe might have been the sexiest men she'd ever known, but nothing, *nothing* was hotter than seeing them at ease with their own desires.

"And what happens when you're done watching?" Rafe asked.

Mikey didn't answer. Just ran a hand over Rafe's back, sliding it lower until his pelvis made the same involuntary jerk Krissy's did.

Rafe shuddered. "Oh, fuck yes."

Hooking her heels firmly over his ass, he carried Krissy to the bed and laid her down beneath him.

"You packed the lube?" Mikey asked as he pulled his shirt off.

Rafe groaned. "Inside pocket of my bag."

Then Rafe kissed her. Pushed her sweatshirt up and tugged it off, her bottoms next, his own clothes too. He slipped her glasses off her face, then reached for Mikey's.

"Guess I'd better get used to this," Rafe said with a smile, but after he'd placed both pairs on the nightstand, he looked down at her with reverence. Asking her permission.

Every inch of her nerve endings was on fire when she said, "Make me fly, Rafe."

Mikey climbed onto the bed and handed over a condom. When Rafe took it from him, Mikey slid a hand over her hip, then stroked downward, testing her slickness with a swipe over her clit and the plunge of a single finger. Rafe knelt between her legs, and Mikey made himself comfortable, pulling his hand back and propping himself up on the other. Krissy sucked back a breath when Rafe pressed inside her, one perfect inch at a time.

"Krissy," he said softly, his forehead sinking down to meet her collarbone.

Mikey hummed approvingly, one hand in his briefs, fist making lazy strokes beneath the fabric. Rafe took one look at Mikey and bit off a moan, then focused back on her as he started to move.

He didn't rush, sliding in and out in long, deep thrusts Krissy couldn't help but rise up to meet. It felt so good—Rafe finally inside her, Mikey by their side, his grin wide like it was Christmas Day.

She urged him faster. Rafe choked out a grunt. "Slow down, sweetheart. I'm not gonna last if you keep that up."

Mikey rose to his knees, eyes flashing. "That's the idea."

Krissy quivered, her insides going molten over his words even as her heart swelled. It was something they'd all said at one point —each of them wanting to get the others off, to drive them wild, dredging up their kinkiest desires and reveling in the aftermath. But what the three of them were about to give each other wasn't just sex. It was everything.

Mikey shed the rest of his clothes and positioned himself at the foot of the bed. Rafe's thrusts slowed even more at the sound of the lube bottle popping open and the rip of another condom wrapper. He cursed and shivered, his breath washing hot along Krissy's neck. Over Rafe's shoulder, she caught a look of absolute concentration on Mikey's face, the subtle movements of his shoulder as his arm flexed. She could hear the wet noises of his finger moving.

"Tell me if it's too much," Mikey said. "Don't want to hurt you."

"Not gonna—*ohh*." Rafe's moan vibrated through her. He slid his arms under hers to grip the pillow. The mattress dipped, and

Krissy's lungs went tight with anticipation as she spread her legs wider.

"Good thing I've got all that dance training," she teased. "Super flexibility."

Rafe laughed against her cheek. "Just, hold still a minute," he pleaded. "You feel so good, you both feel so...oh God."

He pinched his eyes shut and panted out several breaths, his head bowing with the unmistakable pleasure of Mikey easing inside him.

"Shit...I can't believe...so fucking *tight*," Mikey said. Then, more quietly, "You okay?"

The rough timbre of his voice had Krissy grasping at Rafe's back, nails digging into his skin in her effort not to move. Mikey's hands were on Rafe's waist, their legs all entwined, the three of them holding still and trembling.

Rafe nodded. "Stay with me, Mikey." Every inch of him was shaking when he slid his hips back and exhaled. "Okay. Move, both of you, now."

He rolled into her again, and after a few jerky thrusts and whispered curses, the three of them found a rhythm.

Their noises were a harmony of pleasure, Krissy's high-pitched whimpers offset by masculine groans, sensual *mmm*s and *oh yeah*s that switched when one of them arched forward and the other dragged out. The combination of all their body heat had sweat pooling along Krissy's thighs and in the crevices behind her knees, their bodies so close that every tilt of Rafe's hips put pressure on her clit. She needed more direct contact to come, but her release took a backseat when Mikey started moving faster and Rafe's hand flew backward to grasp Mikey's.

"Don't," Rafe said sharply. "It's too good, I'm gonna—" His jaw dropped open, his thrusts going fast and sloppy. "Damn it. Mikey, Krissy...*fuck*."

He went rigid, his shoulders hiking up to his ears as he

moaned. One hard shake of his entire torso, and he collapsed against her.

"Sorry," he said meekly, then kissed her cheek. "Thank you."

"Love you," she whispered back.

Rafe's hiss was the sign of Mikey pulling out of him. He rolled to Krissy's side, his breathing still fast when he glanced up at Mikey.

Mikey's face was flushed, his smile sly and bright, looking positively exhilarated over what he'd done. The two men shared a quick kiss, then Rafe disposed of his condom and handed Mikey a fresh foil package.

God, yes. Mikey went back on his heels and switched condoms with shaky hands.

"Get her ready for me, Rafe."

"Oh, she's ready," he drawled, a bit of that southern accent creeping back in as he palmed her belly. His fingers dipped and swirled, one pinky swiping lower to graze her back entrance. "Maybe one day Mikey and I will take you together. What would you think of that?"

She panted, writhing from Rafe's touch and the idea that they'd be doing this again. That a future of this was ahead of her. "One day."

Mikey braced his arms on either side of her. His hair flopped over his eyes as he hovered over her, sunlight coming in the window and making a halo on the crown of his head.

"I love you," he said. "I'm so happy you came."

Pure delight. No other words for it. "I love you too. But I haven't *come* yet."

He gave her a snarky grin. "I think we can fix that."

There was no preamble, just him filling her and starting a quick pounding, speeding them both toward the edge. Rafe drew Krissy's arms over her head, anchoring them to the pillow with one hand as he read her body's cues with the other, rubbing fast.

"A week of pure deviance," he mused. "Who would've thought it could end in love."

Krissy let go and they caught her, Mikey swallowing both their moans with a kiss.

When they'd curled up on either side of her and had panted back to quiet, Mikey sat up and looked around the room. "There's one more thing I need from you guys before you leave."

Krissy quirked an eyebrow at Rafe. "What's that?"

"We've got a ton of laundry to do."

FOURTEEN

*A*pril 20th: *Feeling excited today, and a little nervous. Can't wait to see Mikey.*

Krissy saved the journal entry on her phone and looked out the airplane window. The landing pattern into Portland Jetport had taken them over the Atlantic, and she'd smiled as soon as she saw the coast dotted with boats, blue water sparkling in the early morning sun.

Her phone buzzed with a text.

You landed yet?

Rafe checking on her, even from hundreds of miles away. *Just got in. Quick flight too. Only a little over an hour.*

It had seemed silly, flying north out of LaGuardia just to turn around and drive back south, but she hadn't wanted Mikey to travel all the way to New York alone.

Good. Give Mikey a kiss for me. Bring him home safely.

She sent back a kiss emoticon and pocketed her phone. The tour was in the Midwest now but would be on the East Coast next month. She and Mikey already had tickets to a Pennsylvania show.

Her heart raced as the plane stopped and the passengers disembarked. Krissy took several calming breaths. It was different, having positive feelings to combat the anxiety. Now that she'd found a new balance of meds, remembering how she'd been before was like looking through a dirty window. Muddy, with every day pulling her forward in a blur of words and gravity, her thoughts too loud for her to hear herself.

She'd learned how to start listening.

The journal was one of the new habits she'd started once she switched therapists. No more mood app or check-ins with her parents. Now she was responsible for keeping track of her own thoughts, but her parents had a login to the diary, agreeing to only use it if it looked like she was slipping. She'd started a new treatment called EMDR, a psychotherapy involving sound and light to help manage her triggers.

She'd also stopped avoiding the word crazy. Fearing a word didn't help her deal with it, and she'd sent her old college roommate a long email to explain what had happened, discovering the power in taking ownership for her actions. Dance had replaced yoga—she'd begun training once again at her childhood ballet studio, and she'd tiptoed back into acting by giving voice lessons and doing some community theater. NYU was on hold until the fall, and she'd be taking it slow. No full course loads, and a part-time job to bring balance to her life.

And when she had trouble finding it, she had Rafe and Mikey.

She sprinted out of the gate, her carry-on over her shoulder. As she raced toward baggage claim, she could make out Mikey's form in the crowd. His grin widened as she got closer, and then he was scooping her up in his arms and twirling her around. He kissed her before she had a chance to say a word, and she laughed when their glasses clicked together.

"I missed you so much," he breathed against her mouth.

"Me too." She passed a hand through his hair. The floppy locks were now layered and spiked, the round frames he'd worn traded for more fashionable ones. "Rafe's gonna love this cut."

He blushed. "You've both already seen it."

"Not in real life."

Three-way Skype calls several times a week had kept them connected. Not all of them had been PG-13. Mikey had gotten *really* comfortable with the whole voyeurism thing.

He clasped her hand and led her outside. A U-Haul truck waited in the short-term lot.

"Okay, let me see it," she said as soon as they slid in the cab.

Mikey lifted the sleeve of his shirt, revealing a smaller version of Rafe's tattoo on his upper arm. Krissy clapped and then hiked up her pant leg. The same design was on her ankle.

Mikey fingers were light over the image drawn on her skin. "He's going to love these."

It had been Mikey's idea to get the ink—something they could share to honor the innocent and deviant in all of them, and show their commitment to one another. They'd kept it a surprise, wanting to show Rafe in person next month.

"I hope so," she said. "You look ridiculously sexy, by the way."

It wasn't just the tatt, the new do, or the glasses, or the stubble he'd let grow along his jaw. Mikey had grown into himself somehow in the last four and a half months, turning into a happier, more secure version of the guy he'd been.

"You always look sexy." Mikey ran his fingers through her hair, now dyed back to its original jet black, and put the truck in drive.

When they arrived at his house, Mikey's friends and parents were waiting. Even though he'd been paying the Queens apartment's rent since January, he'd chosen not to move right away, transitioning his students to a new instructor and helping his parents with the remainder of winter. Spring could still mean plenty of snow for southern Maine, but he'd gotten a job, and it was time.

"So tell me about this new gig," Dean said as they started heaving boxes into the truck. "You're like some kind of Jesus Christ Superstar?"

"You know that show?" Krissy asked.

Jamie cackled. The large box she was carrying was labeled *books* but her swimmer's arms could handle it. "He became a huge fan of Broadway when we were in New York. I think he might want to go back and visit more than I do."

Mikey shoved his bike to the far corner of the truck, his guitar case nestled next to it.

"I'm the musical director at a Progressive Christian church. It's paying, because I'll be working with the kids as well as the adult choir. I'll be doing outreach too, volunteering at an inner-city school to work in their community garden."

Krissy's heart swelled. It had taken some time, but Mikey had found a way to combine the things he was passionate about. He'd also come to the decision that God wasn't only found in the Catholic Church or the Bible. God was everywhere—in nature. In music. In laughter.

In love.

"And what about your roommate?" Dean asked Krissy. "He looking for a new place now that you guys'll be moving in?"

Mikey put an arm around Krissy. "No."

His simple and confident answer had Krissy blushing and leaning into his side. Dean's brows crept upward as he and Connor exchanged surprised and amused looks. Off to the side, Jamie, and Connor's fiancée, Gabriella, grinned widely.

Connor cleared his throat. "Damn, Mikey. Didn't know you had it in you."

They returned to packing, stopping when Mikey's parents brought in lunch. They sat down at the table together, a final meal before hitting the road. Mikey hadn't told his parents about Rafe, although he'd hinted at it. It wasn't something they needed to know yet. Krissy had plans to explain things to her family with her therapist present. She wouldn't be sharing all the details— just that come summer, she'd be moving in with two men who made her incredibly happy.

It was the middle of the afternoon by the time they'd finishing loading the truck. An eight-hour drive was ahead of them. Rafe had prepared a playlist to keep her and Mikey alert, as well as to "do something about Mikey's taste in music", as he'd put it. Krissy plugged her phone into portable speakers and cued up the first song. Lady Gaga's "Born This Way" started playing.

Dean coughed out a laugh. "Least it's better than country."

Oh yeah. When the time came, he and Rafe would get along just fine.

She and Mikey exchanged quick hugs with his parents, Krissy promising to let them know when they'd reached their destination. Gabriella embraced Krissy with a warm squeeze, something Krissy wouldn't have expected given the fact that they'd met that morning.

"We'll see you all in July for the wedding, right?" Gabriella asked.

"Of course." Mikey was one of Connor's groomsmen. And *all* implied that Krissy and Rafe would be invited too. "Wouldn't miss it."

The guys hugged quickly—manly holds that ended with a few hard slaps on the back—before Krissy and Mikey headed for the cab. Jamie told Krissy not to be a stranger, then tucked herself against Dean's shoulder. Connor pulled Gabriella close, and the four of them waved from the driveway as Mikey backed down it.

"They're really nice," Krissy said when he started down the

road. "I feel a little bad that Rafe and I are stealing you away from them."

"Don't worry. You're not stealing anything." He smiled as he glanced in the side-view mirror. "I'll always be one of the Portland rebels."

The Theory of Deviance was never meant to be comfortable. Writing Krissy, Mikey, and Rafe meant leaning into desire that doesn't behave, love that refuses labels, and the messy truth that wanting something doesn't make it wrong.

If this story pushed you outside your comfort zone, lingered with you longer than expected, or surprised you with how emotional it became, I'd love to hear your thoughts. Reviews help books like this reach readers who are willing to sit with complexity, vulnerability, and unconventional connections.

If you feel inclined, you can leave a review wherever you purchased the book, or on Goodreads. Even a few honest lines help more than you might think.

 *Rebecca Grace Allen*

ALSO BY REBECCA GRACE ALLEN

Legally Bound:

His Contract

Her Claim

Their Discovery

Portland Rebels:

The Duality Principle

The Hierarchy of Needs

Shakespeare in the City:

Taming Sugar

Hunter Pains

Decades Duet:

Find the Cost of Freedom

Smells Like Teen Spirit

About the Author

Rebecca lives in southern Florida with three cats who firmly believe they are the main characters. When she's not immersed in fictional love stories, she can usually be found chasing strong coffee, good workouts, and the kind of books that balance heart, heat, and humor. She writes romance for readers who like their happily ever afters earned, their characters flawed, and their love stories a little messy in the best possible way.